PLAYED

STAR BREED: BOOK EIGHT

ELIN WYN

AEDAN

"The funny thing is, if they had bothered cutting Granny Z in on the deal, she probably would've given them her blessing." Kara's eyes gleamed as she reviewed the piles of merchandise scattered before us.

"That's a terrible idea," I muttered. "We're supposed to be a force for good on the Fringe, legitimacy, something like that, right?"

"I think we've got a ways to go before we have to worry about being too much of a glittering beacon of civilization, Aedan," she waved her arm at the station deck below us.

Since Lorcan had arrived back with Cintha, the Pack had made a steady push to clear out the last of the human traffickers, criminal gangs, and other assorted scum from Orem Station. Cintha's connections with the kid gangs had been invaluable, leading right to the arms smuggling ring we'd shut down tonight.

Despite myself, I shuddered. Too much punch in a laser on a space station was a bad idea. And those idiots had been moving high-frequency cannons to the highest bidder.

"Humans. What the hell were they thinking?"

Kara shot me an odd look over the tablet she was using. "You know Doc is fully human, right?"

"Are you sure?" I shot back.

"Yes," she answered. "You're just grumpy because that big bald guy bled all over you when you took him down." Her eyes narrowed. "Are you getting soft?"

"I can get as rough as any of the others," I growled. "But this was my favorite shirt."

Kara laughed. "You know the replicator can make you a dozen more just like it, right?"

"Of course. But that's not the point."

And it wasn't. That shirt was broken in to just the right softness. I liked it.

After years of missions in every hellhole of the Fringe, a little softness was nice.

Nothing wrong with having a favorite shirt.

"Well," Kara tilted her chin back to where the station guards were processing the prisoners. "Maybe one of those fellows can tell you where to find another shirt that has whatever mystical qualities they ruined in that one."

Whatever.

We were done here. The station guards could wrap it up. They didn't need me anymore, and I couldn't wait to get some dinner and a shower.

I pulled off the ruined shirt, leaving on the vest to cover my chest, and stomped ahead.

Not too fast, though.

Kara didn't even bother to try to match my pace. "You need to learn how to take a little teasing, Aedan."

"No, I don't." But I stopped and waited for her to catch up.

She patted my arm. "I'm fine down here, you know, sort of reminds me of home."

Kara looked around at the dark warren before us, the muted reds and orange of the pleasure district far away from this corner of the Under.

Here, there was nothing but grime, crime and corruption.

"Davien would skin me alive if I left you by yourself in the Under," I muttered.

"Ah, well..." a bit of pink came to her copper cheeks. "How about we don't mention that I was with you this time?"

"What?"

She kept walking with barely a shrug. "He gets worried too easily. I'm not really built to stay safe."

Kara spat out the word as if she'd tasted something foul. "Honestly, ever since we came here, he's been getting all… official. It's not really my scene."

"I can believe that," I said, running quickly through my options. "But could that issue be settled between you and Davien, and leave me out of it?"

"That's why I gave you a heads-up," she replied, nudging my shoulder. "We're family. I wouldn't want to get you into trouble unnecessarily."

Family.

I thought about it as we climbed through the layers of Orem Station until we emerged at one of the residential zones of the Lowers.

"I'm going to pop out here, check on Eris." Kara announced, her voice tight. "If this doesn't work out…"

I put a hand on her shoulder. "Doc says everything is fine. We've got to trust her."

She snorted. "Trust Doc? Because she knows so much about how babies are usually made. Sure."

Her face softened and for a moment, I could see how worried she really was under that tough veneer.

About Eris, about the baby that still hadn't arrived yet.

About everything.

"Anyhow. Not a word to Davien about this, okay? Think of it as a favor to a sister."

She disappeared, and I wandered out of the residential zone and into the Bazaar, looking for food.

Residents of Orem nodded, stepping out of my way. People who lived here knew enough not to be worried about my presence, but they also knew I wasn't the most talkative of my brothers.

My brothers.

Sisters now, too, apparently.

Our family.

Was that really what we were?

We've been bred this way, trained together, formed into a fighting force stronger than permasteel, but did that actually make us a family?

My order came up, a trio of pale fluffy balls, still moist from the steamer, hiding shredded spicy veg and protein inside.

And then my comm pinged, louder than the grumbling of my stomach.

"Aedan, report to Command." Davien's voice sounded in my ear, sounding just as curt as usual.

Void take it.

Maybe one of the human guards had already said something about Kara being on that mission.

Family indeed.

Not sure if any of it was worth it.

MYRIA

"Easy, girl," I crooned to Dayla as she picked her way through the crowded streets of Trandor.

Not one of the more shining cities I'd ever visited in my travels, but honestly, few of them were.

Holding my satchel a little closer to me, I leaned forward from my precarious perch to scratch in her favorite spot, right between the green and yellow stripes that covered Dayla's pebbled hide above her short forearms.

"Almost to the end, and then you'll have a nice bundle of leaves," I promised as her long legs carried us through the winding,; muck-covered streets.

We caught a few glares and stares, as usual.

Some people could manage to bond enough with a torwynn to last a season or two. Most didn't manage, instead relying on the heavier zugrin to draw carts and wagons.

Torwynn required more dedication. And certainly more conversation.

I had a theory. Actually, I'd heard about it from a half-drunk grizzled old man in a bar.

You'd be surprised how much information I picked up from half-drunk grizzled old men in bars.

But back to the theory.

It seemed like there was a season in their lifespans during which torwynn wanted to explore the world, leave the herd and wander.

But they preferred to do it in company - either with a member of their herd, or another herd passing by, or even, if they weren't too picky, a human.

I had found Dayla far from any other herd, curiously picking at low hanging norvell branches.

Considering even then she was twice my height, I felt justified in being a bit nervous about approaching.

But the distance I could cover on torwynn-back was enough of an incentive to spur me on, bring me closer.

She didn't strike with her talons, didn't bounce away on those absurdly long, backwards-hinged legs.

She just lowered her head and stared at me with glossy black eyes as if to say, "Where have you been? Scratch this eye ridge. Get on that."

We'd traveled together for two years now, and I

wondered how much longer it would be before she felt the stirring to return to her herd.

"Things are getting interesting, old girl," I murmured. "Stay with me a little longer, all right?"

She chuffed in answer.

And as usual, I read into it whatever I wanted.

We were halfway to a tavern I had worked at before when the crowd suddenly thinned out.

I frowned. That wasn't good. Whatever was up ahead was scaring the locals away. Locals that I needed to be happy and relaxed, spending their money in the tavern.

Not too nervous to walk the streets.

It didn't take long to figure out the problem.

A small group of men walked boldly down the middle of the street, wearing the black and orange coats that marked them as Flame's elite guard.

They surrounded a young man with bruises clear on his face, shackles on his wrists.

What the hell were they doing here?

Flame's citadel was at least two days' travel away, and that was pushing it.

The locals scattered at the sight of them, not wanting to risk confrontation.

I didn't blame them.

Even if this was borderland territory, Flame's soldiers could travel just as freely as a bard.

But no one liked them.

"They like us a little bit, at least, don't they, Dayla?"

She didn't even chuff.

In a small berg like this, no one wanted anything to do with Flame's boys if they could help it.

Including me.

As the band approached, a dark-haired man in the lead fixed me with a pointed stare.

"We're as far to the side as we can get, jackass," I muttered.

His eyes felt oily on my skin and I let out a sigh of relief as they passed by.

Once they were out of sight, the crowd resumed its regular movements and Dayla and I picked our way through the muck to the tavern, thick smoke pouring from its chimney.

In a bigger town, the Red Thrall would look run-down, beat-up.

Here, it fit in with the rest of the town.

I wasn't going to make a lot of money here, but there were other things than money that were worthwhile.

You wouldn't think it to look at it, but from my previous trip through, I knew they actually had a good setup for torwynn here, with stalls tall enough to accommodate their towering height, and piles and piles of norvell branches.

Of course, they'd mostly be expecting zugrin, but enough travelers came through that the stable hand would know what to do with Dayla.

Unrolling the short rope ladder from the saddle, I swung my leg over and climbed down, careful not to catch the bow on my back on any of her rigging.

A lean girl with her hair in a rat's nest but clean-enough leathers stepped forward.

"She gonna give me any trouble taking the harness off?"

"No," I answered, as I scratched down the side of Dayla's pebbled muzzle. "She's the sweetest-tempered torwynn I've ever met."

The girl stared at me, unimpressed. "They all say that." Nevertheless, she stepped forward and led Dayla into a pen that looked cleaner than anything else I'd seen in this town.

When I slipped inside the smoke-filled tavern, a slow grin crawled across my face.

Unlike the smoke outside, this wasn't from a cook fire, but was the easy, thick smoke of hash.

The scent made my nose crinkle, and for the sake of my throat and my brain, I'd have to stay away from the worst of it.

But it meant there was a little extra coin for pleasures here. And plenty of people who would be feeling relaxed, ready to talk, gossip.

Who knew what news I could pick up?

Behind the bar, a sturdy looking woman with her hair in long rows of braids watched me.

"Passing through?"

I slid my retrew carefully from its carrying case in my satchel.

"Hoping to play for a night or two, if you'll have me."

I'd be shocked if she wouldn't.

Since the so-called peace, the only way news spread from town to town was by travelers, the rumor network, and bards.

The thought still made me laugh.

Here we were, theoretically part of some great intergalactic Empire.

But the Emperor had cast us off, and due to greed and anger, the whole planet had been turned into something straight out of a history book.

My great-grandmother remembered the war, and the change…the soldiers coming through, confiscating every weapon, every bit of tech.

She'd never forgotten.

Never forgiven.

Not the warlords, and not the Emperor.

"Can't pay'ya," the woman said flatly. "But I can feed you, get you space in the storeroom to sleep."

"Take care of me and my mount, and we're all square," I promised.

I stuck my hand out, shook hers, and listened to the hum of the tavern.

Not quite full.

"More folks coming in later?" I asked.

She nodded. "A bit after dark is when they mostly come by."

That would do.

That would do just fine.

AEDAN

Ronan and Nadira had left to navigate Hub politics a week ago. Something to do with the Council, and trade agreements. Didn't know, didn't really care.

Nadira would navigate things, and Ronan would destroy anyone who was in her way.

And Davien was left to handle station security.

He wasn't exactly thrilled about it, which meant we all suffered.

But Davien wasn't the only one waiting for me in the control room.

"There he is!" gushed a rich male voice as I came into the office.

Oh no.

I've been so busy carefully not-thinking about Kara's words that I hadn't picked up the scent.

A tall male, immaculately dressed in crimson and white, bounced up from one of the plush chairs that Nadira had insisted Ronan's office needed.

They were especially useful when people walked in for the first time. Command was deep in the heart of Orem Station, but we'd fixed screens over all the walls.

Sometimes they showed data for specific missions, or cam-feeds from decks where trouble had been reported.

But most of the time, they showed exactly what you'd see if you weren't in the station. Space.

The ships coming in and out of port.

But mostly, just the deep black.

Which was where I'd like to throw a certain someone.

"Why is he here?" I asked Davien.

"Because I'm the Emperor and can go where I want?" answered Vandalar.

I snapped my head back towards him. "You're not the Emperor yet." A terrible thought struck… "Are you?"

"Actually," the dark blond man dropped back into the chair, the idiotic façade slipping away. "It's going to be soon. Grandfather's faculties are fading, and he knows it."

Davien and I shot each other frowns.

To be trapped in your body, knowing your mind was slowly leaving, betraying you. It was the worst nightmare for all of us.

"If anything, the business with General Melchior has made him more determined than ever to step aside early."

Vandalar rubbed his eyes and I noticed the strained, fine lines around the outer corners that told of more sleepless nights than human men were designed for.

"But he wants everyone around for the big day."

"We're not going," Davien said flatly.

Vandalar laughed, low and long, finally tipping his head back to rest against the back of the chair.

"Oh no, that's not what he meant. Not at all. But thank you. I just had the most pleasing vision of all of you stopping in, glowering until the court finally fell silent."

"No," Davien growled.

"Still, I'll treasure the imagined memory."

"So, what do you want?" I snapped.

What *I* wanted was a shower, to get a fresh order of steamed buns and actually get to eat them this time.

To stop dancing around things with this loser.

Vandalar's face turned stern, possibly almost regal.

"I need you to find my aunt," Vandalar answered.

"My great-aunt Eladia, really. My grandfather's favorite sister. She's gone missing."

"It's a big galaxy out there," I leaned back in my chair, thinking wistfully of dinner. "Missing doesn't really give us much to go on."

"Believe it or not, I'm not an idiot," said Vandalar.

"It'd be easier to remember if you stopped acting it," said Davien.

"Maybe you can have that interesting AI of yours remind me every time I enter Orem," Vandalar said dryly. "I've heard it's remarkably useful."

I could do that, chirped Nixie.

Void. She'd been listening to the whole thing.

"Nixie, everything that's ever said in this room is private, you understand that, right?" I demanded of the air, to wherever Nixie had decided to place her interfaces.

"Except for family, you mean, right?"

"It may be the best you get," Davien shot at Vandalar.

"That's fine," Vandalar waved dismissively. "I don't understand your family, but it's no crazier than mine."

"Ask Eris before you tell anyone else," Davien clarified the order. "Make sure Eris thinks they're okay to know."

I can do that, I can do that right now, I'm doing that while we're talking.

Of course she could.

And I've put in a reminder notice so that every time your ship comes in, it will get a special surprise! Won't it be fun?

Vandalar looked nervous.

We probably all did.

"That's great," he said weakly.

"So, tell us more about this aunt of yours," Davien sighed. "When did she go missing and why?"

"And what do you want us to do about it?" I threw in.

"Here's what I have." Vandalar tossed a tablet to me.

Despite myself, my eyebrows rose.

"A ransom demand?"

"A very specific one, yes."

"Someone apparently feels they don't have anything to lose."

"All, of course, couched in the politest of phrases," Vandalar snarled. "But yes, they're holding the Princess Eladia hostage."

I kept scrolling through the list of demands. "Whoever this Flame character is, he seems to want quite a lot." I scrolled further.

"Mostly weapons, you'll notice." Vandalar commented dryly.

"How do you even know he's got her?" Davien asked.

"We know it's her because he was kind enough to send a tissue sample. Apparently, he means business."

I tapped the side of the commtab. “No way it could have been grown or cloned, or any of the usual methods?”

Vandalar threw his hands in the air. “Of course it could have been. But it doesn’t seem likely that a warlord on a backwater Fringe planet would have access to my great-aunt’s cells to even start the cloning process enough for a sample.”

Davien shrugged. “Fair point.”

“I still don’t understand why you want us involved.” I leaned back in the chair, stretched a little, and watched a small merchant-class ship leave the dock. “If you’re about to be the Emperor, couldn’t you deploy a few hundred of those fancy guards of yours, take over the place, scour it to the ground until you find her?”

“I could.” Vandalar’s expression changed, making it clear that this time, I was the idiot. “But as you might have noticed from trying to keep a single space station in line, every time you solve one problem, another pops up.” He turned to watch the ship slowly move away before its engines caught and it streaked into a jump.

“At the moment, I’m working on solidifying my control of the capital, making personal visitations throughout the Hub, and making sure that all of our alliances and governors aren’t going to start another rebellion.”

"We'd appreciate that," Davien replied. "The last one nearly took us out."

Vandalar bowed his head and continued. "Kerrind has been off the Imperial radar for almost one hundred years. The only contact we've had with them was before I was born. One of their warlords came to court asking for weapons."

He ran his hand through his hair.

"My grandfather sent them away without an audience. I don't think it was the best idea. Apparently, they spent the next couple of generations tied up in a civil war that sent them more or less back to the Stone Age."

Vandalar tossed a data chip to Davien, who threw the data up on the screen.

Maps, flight paths, population data.

All probably horribly out of date.

And he didn't care.

"I want this done discreetly. Go in. Find my great-aunt, and get her out of there."

I looked at Davien, still bewildered. "I still don't know why any of your team can't do it."

"Did I mention that part about them going back to the Stone Age?" Vandalar snapped. "Maybe that's a bit much. But as part of the truce between the warlords, all hi-tech has been forbidden." He rubbed his eyes. "Everything that would be helpful to any of my men would mark them immediately as an outsider."

"Or belonging to one of the warlords," I added. "You know whoever they are is keeping the good stuff for themselves."

"That might be true," Vandalar nodded. "But that still doesn't help me. If at all possible, I want to avoid upsetting the peace they've gained there. Ideally, I'd have someone on the ground who could make a report on the situation, advise on how to bring them back into the Imperial fold."

"Good luck with that," I said. "Sounds like the place is ready to be all kinds of upset no matter what you do."

He raised one eyebrow. "It'll be more upset if my great-aunt isn't at the rehearsal for the coronation in ten days. So far, we've kept Eladia's disappearance a secret from my grandfather, but once he learns of it, all bets are off. He'll take half the navy and lay waste to that Flame's stronghold until he gets her back."

"Well, then you wouldn't have to deal with Kerrind and its problems at all," Davien offered. "Sounds like there wouldn't be enough of them left to cause you trouble for another generation or two."

"That's not exactly how I'd like to handle it," Vandalar muttered. "I think the only one who could get my aunt out of there without sparking another war would be one of Lyall's Wolves."

Davien looked at me and I groaned.

Getting a new shirt would have to wait.

MYRIA

After a quick check on Dayla and a promise of stew and homemade bread later, I found a corner to set up in, and started with some slow, soft music, just to get myself warmed up.

The chatter in the bar died down slightly as everyone turned their attention to me. It didn't seem like too many bards came through here.

Which just meant more gossip for me.

Once the novelty wore off for most patrons, the chatter picked up again. I closed my eyes and opened my ears, my body playing on pure muscle memory now.

Words slipped from my lips on autopilot, a simple ballad that served as nothing more than background noise for most of the patrons now.

Which meant they'd all resumed their conversations and I could slowly start to pick up bits and pieces of them.

So far, it was mostly just the basic back and forth, people talking about their days, their families. Even in these poor towns, people still had regular lives, lives not so different from the richer towns and taverns.

Kids got sick, spouses had arguments, people had issues at work.

One of the things you realized as a musician was how much humanity was universal, at least across this world.

I played a few more songs as the bar started to fill up. Bits and pieces of information reached my ears, but none of it was very special.

The comings and goings of the town didn't seem to be very hot today, at least not that anyone was talking about so far. That could very easily change once the night went on and people had a bit more to drink.

Hash and alcohol, even the mediocre stuff served here, helped loosen lips.

Things people would never dream of talking about sober would start pouring from their lips.

After a couple more songs, the tavern owner caught my attention.

Dinner was ready, and it was time for a break. When

I sat down at the bar, people looked my way, but few actually paid me any attention.

They were used to me now. Just the bard in the corner.

I was invisible.

It meant I could enjoy my meal in peace and quiet. It also meant I could listen to what everyone around me was saying, since they tended to speak as if I wasn't there.

Which was even better.

"Here you go," a burly older man said as he put a steaming bowl of stew in front of me, with thick slices of brown bread to the side. "Bread baked this afternoon. Some of my best loaves."

I glanced up, surprised. "You're the baker?"

"We worked it out years ago," he grinned from behind a thick, dark beard. "I'm happier in the kitchen, and she's better in the front. Besides, people think I'm scary. That's not good for business."

He tapped the bowl. "Let me know if you need more." Then he disappeared back into the kitchen.

Whatever arrangement the owners had come up with, I couldn't argue. The food was delicious, hot and filling.

A couple of women sat not too far from me at the end of the bar. They both had drinks in their hands and were grinning at each other, probably enjoying a much-needed night out.

"I'm tellin' ya, Dabins saw the most peculiar thing the other day," the one woman said, her accent thick. Born and raised in this little town, I imagined.

"He was over in Lukin, delivering a load of barrels, and a great spaceship came down, just as normal as you please."

The other woman scoffed. "Had he been drinking the cargo? Nothing lands at Lukin, or anywhere else."

The first woman opened her mouth to argue, but before I could hear what she said, a meaty hand fell on my shoulder.

I turned to glare at the man, coming face to face with an orange and black coat.

A quick glance up confirmed what I feared.

It was the man from earlier, the one I'd seen walking down the street at the head of Flame's men, terrifying the locals.

His men were occupying a corner to themselves, everyone else staying far away.

Now if only he'd stayed far away from me, I thought to myself.

"Can I help you?" I asked, fighting to keep my tone even. I wanted to pushed him away and tell him to fuck off, but that wasn't exactly the polite thing to do.

And in my line of work, politeness paid.

For all I knew, he'd liked my performance and wanted to give me a tip.

No sense in biting his head off just yet.

The man grinned at me, quirking an eyebrow. It was a look I'd seen on dozens of men before, the look of someone who'd had way too much to drink and had way too much confidence in his meager ability.

"I'm Kaljak," he said, his voice slightly slurred. I didn't think he'd been in here long, but apparently, he'd been hitting the brew hard.

Either that or he was a bigger lightweight than I was.

"Can I help you with something, Kaljak?" I said dryly. "Did you want to request a song?"

His grin slipped for a moment.

Apparently, he wasn't used to people not jumping at the chance to get into his pants. In moments, though, his surprise had vanished and the grin was back.

"Why don't you come back over to my place for the night? I bet I can compensate you better than this run-down tavern."

Turning back toward the bar, I downed the rest of my drink before sliding off the stool.

"Thanks, but no thanks," I said simply before walking off and leaving him there.

I could feel his gaze boring into me as I headed back over to my alcove.

The women who'd been talking about the ship had moved on to other topics, and no matter how curious I was, it seemed rude to interrupt them and ask about something I'd been eavesdropping on.

I'd get more information about it later.

For now, it was time to get back to work.

The moment I started playing again, I had all eyes on me. There was still a dull murmur going through the bar, but both the music and my voice carried clearly through the room as I sang about an epic battle from the war, a classic tale I'd learned early.

It was a favorite in taverns like this, and patrons usually eagerly awaited the song, since every singer performed the ballad differently.

By the time I finished, everyone seemed to be grinning, raising their glasses in support. I was riding a high now, feeding off the crowd's energy.

Until I noticed him, sitting at a table at the front of the crowd, watching me just a little too intently.

I looked away quickly, but there was no mistaking the dark heat in Kaljak's eyes.

For some stupid reason, he'd decided to obsess.

About me.

I started another song, but a shadow fell across the floor as Kaljak strode towards me.

"Don't you think it's time for another break?" The leer was unmistakable.

"Nope." I leaned away, but he pulled at my arm, loosening my grip on the retrew.

And that was it.

"Back off!" I snapped. "I don't know what you think you're doing, but I'm working here!"

"I know, I just can't resist that magical voice of yours," Kaljak smirked, tugging me towards him.

"Hey now," the burly baker hurried out from behind the counter, four more townsmen at his side. "Leave the bard alone. Even Flame's man should know better than that."

Kaljak glanced at the rest of his men, then the townsmen arranging themselves, ready for a fight.

"This is private business, old man."

"We don't have any business," I argued, pulling away. "I'm not interested."

Kaljak's face reddened, then grew carefully blank.

"Whatever. I don't need to waste my time on a whore like you."

He stomped away, his men following him.

I looked up to the tavern owner. "Sorry if I cost you business."

He shrugged. "His kind never expects to pay, anyway."

Despite Flame's men leaving, the air was still thick with tension. Hurriedly I strummed a few notes, starting a round of old favorites, easy, popular songs that everyone could sing along with.

By the fourth verse, people were slapping each other's backs, smiling and happy again, tossing a few coins into my upturned cap.

The incident with Flame's men was forgotten.

But I knew better.

Entitled assholes like Kaljak didn't forget.

After the crowd had dispersed, I slid upstairs to grab my pack. I looked wistfully at the mattress. It would've been nice to sleep in a bed for a change.

But it'd be nicer not to have to sleep with one ear alert for a heavy step on the stair.

The stable hand wasn't too happy about being woken up in the middle of the night. With a sigh, I gave her more of my earnings than I'd planned.

"I'll get her harnessed myself," I said. "But, let me know if you see anybody around, would you?"

Face twisted in a scowl, she headed off, making a circuit of the tavern by the time I had prepared Dayla.

"No one around," she said. "I heard you picked up something of an admirer."

"Picked up, and hoping to scrape off," I answered as I climbed up to Dayla's back.

"Catch you next time I'm through," I called over my shoulder as Dayla and I headed towards the edge of town.

Bitters was the next closest stop, not too far across the open desert.

Not exactly a sprawling city, but bigger than this one.

I'd be able to lose myself there if necessary.

This wasn't the first time I might need to disappear.

Likely it wouldn't be my last.

I let myself slip into a half-doze, rocking with Dayla's easy pace. As dawn crept across the desert, I stopped long enough to let her graze.

By the time the sun was midway through the sky, Trandor was long behind me.

Dayla's hearing was far more acute than mine and not once had she shied or bristled in fright.

We plodded along, not in so much of a hurry that I wanted to risk overheating in the desert, but at enough of a clip to make good time across the sand and rocks.

But suddenly Dayla froze, muscles stiff under her pebbled hide.

Turning in the saddle, I saw nothing disturbing the sand that stretched off behind us.

"Ahead of us, then. Come on, sweetheart, let's go take a look."

Cautiously I urged her forward, unhooking my bow and nocking an arrow.

If it was just some desert creature, Dayla would have

ignored it if it wasn't a threat, or altered her path to avoid it.

Humans were the only thing she ever seemed uncertain about.

My gut clenched as we worked around a rocky outcropping.

No one had tech.

That was the rule of the new peace.

But rules were broken with impunity by those in power, and trusted soldiers of a warlord might well have faster transport than a torwynn.

There was a chance that Kaljak had managed to get around me with his men and set up an ambush.

But as we got closer, I could hear what had set Dayla off.

If it was an ambush, it was a terrible one, with all the racket being made.

And then finally I could see.

Not Flame's men, just a band of outlaws, preying on travelers.

I raised my bow, looking for a clear shot.

In theory, my status should have kept me safe.

In practice, I'd rather not leave alive any bandits to prey on another group of innocent travelers.

Except it wasn't a group of travelers.

It was a single man.

But he fought like an army.

Tall and broad, with pale gold hair that caught the sun.

Spinning, throwing kicks and punches so fast I almost couldn't see, a long knife flashing in the light.

A shaggy-haired bandit lunged at him with his sword and in a flash, he twisted it away from the man, thrust it behind him to gut another opponent, then flipped it back around to slit the throat of the one in front of him.

I lowered my bow slightly.

"I don't think he needs our help, do you?" I asked Dayla.

But then I saw it, just a shadow in the rocks above.

Enough to make me take notice, to squint in the morning light, until I saw someone creeping above the besieged fighter.

Dammit.

I was much too far away to be able to shout any sort of coherent warning.

But if I didn't do something, the trap would be complete.

I lifted my bow, taking careful aim.

Slowly, carefully, the bandit crept across the rocks.

And then I let the arrow fly.

AEDAN

I'd been on this rock for less than a day and I already hated it.

The metadata on the ransom comm had placed Princess Eladia's kidnapper in one of the larger settlements to the east.

It was tempting to have the *Queen* drop me in the middle of the town square, storm the castle, rescue the princess, and be gone before anyone knew what had happened.

In theory, that shouldn't start a war, right?

But even in a crappy mood, I knew how to do my job.

So the *Queen* landed me in the middle of the desert in the middle of the night, while Vandalar sent an ongoing stream of messages to this Flame person.

Group.

Whatever.

Everything I had on me was as low-tech as possible. A knife, a set of clothes that matched the images of the last visitors Kerrind had sent to court, and a sack of coins Vandalar swore would be taken as currency.

Not even a commtab, just a burstcomm to trigger once I'd found the hostage.

And if I didn't trigger it in time, well, Vandalar or his grandfather would come for her anyway.

I didn't mind being planet-side as much as some of my brothers did. And it'd been a while since I'd really been able to let myself run.

And then the suns had come up, and shortly afterwards, these jokers decided I looked like an easy target.

Not really a bad thing.

While running had been good to stretch my legs, I'd never argue with the chance to hit someone who deserved it.

And from the way the men swarmed out of the rocks surrounding the trail, it was a safe bet they weren't exactly offering honorable combat to passersby.

The last of them lay in the filthy, bloody heap at my feet when the whirring hum of a projectile caught my attention.

Diving to the side, I rolled, scanning to see what threat I'd missed.

With a hoarse yell, another of the bandits fell from a rocky outcropping right over where I'd been.

The sneak landed with a thud and didn't move.

Striding over to him, I yanked the arrow out and stared at the newcomer.

Actually, first I stared at her mount.

She was riding a dinosaur.

Or something close enough that it didn't matter.

Giant lizards, alternate evolutionary paths of different planets, Doc'd had us watch all the vids.

She figured that especially with our...interesting...natures, we should understand how things like that worked.

Yet still, I'd never really expected to come face to face with a woman perched on the back of what looked like a pint-sized Tyrannosaurus rex.

But there she was.

Dark skin and straight black hair coming loose from a long braid that poked out from a long scarf wrapped around it. She was comfortably holding the bow that I had no doubt had sent the arrow into the attacker.

She waited, watching.

"My thanks," I called out. "But there's no need to get involved."

"Next time, I'll let him get the drop on you," she

answered, her voice low and rich. "Mind giving me my arrow back?"

I walked up to her mount, which shied back.

Void. Not a surprise, altogether.

Some animals seemed to react badly to our scent.

Somehow, I guessed none of us had ever interacted with something like whatever that thing was.

"Easy, Dayla," the woman crooned, leaning forward to scratch her monstrous mount's head.

That close, I could see the differences from the dinosaurs in the old vids.

The flat teeth were obviously not meant for the rending and tearing of flesh, rather for chewing leaves. Or entire branches.

Maybe trees.

Not that I'd seen too many trees here.

"Sorry," the woman said. "Dayla's not always good with strangers, and the sound of the fight startled her. She should be fine now."

"Not a problem," I said. Warily, I reached up, around those teeth, and the woman reached down from her high perch to take the arrow from me.

The wind shifted and for just a moment, I caught her scent.

Springtime, cool water, and fresh flowers, all ran together there in that dusty desert.

I stepped away.

No time for that.

I'll be going now.

She cocked an eyebrow.

"Are you sure? Traveling on your own on foot isn't really the best way to cross the desert."

"Yeah, I'm sure." I turned around and kept heading towards the next town.

It would take a couple hours, but by then, I'd have learned more about this world.

Talked to some people, gathered intel.

Maybe found a band of travelers to infiltrate, use them as cover to … nope. Not happening.

Not her.

Someone else would come along.

"That's not exactly a great idea," she said from behind me as I walked away. "That won't be the only band of outlaws out here."

I started walking faster, moving into a light jog that I could keep up for hours.

Her beast just increased its stride, staying right next to me.

"She thinks you're playing with her," the woman said dryly.

A huff of hot breath washed over me.

"Dayla! Stop it!"

I picked up the pace, only to be lovingly nudged by a muzzle the size of my torso.

"I'm Myria," the woman said, smothering a grin that I didn't need to see to sense. "And I really think you could use a guide."

"I don't need one," I said, insisting again, doing my best to calmly remove myself from Dayla's side.

Apparently, she had only worried about the fact that I was new.

My scent didn't bother her at all.

And to top it all off, she thought my hair was some sort of new, tasty, exciting plant.

"I'm sorry, but could you keep your whatever-the-hell-that-thing-is in order?" I snapped.

She shook her head, "I was pretty sure you were from off-world before. Now I know it."

Void.

"That's ridiculous," I snapped. "Of course I'm not from off-world. How would that even happen?"

Myria laughed, the low smoky sound dancing down my spine like caressing fingers.

"For one thing, your clothes. You stand out, but they scream it. They're all too new, they fit you too well. None of it looks like it was woven here."

Myria gasped and I whirled, ready for another threat.

All was well, but her eyes were wide as she said with awe, "Don't tell me those are from a replicator?"

Somehow, this hadn't been in my field notes for the mission.

"Of course not," I answered quickly and turned around to keep walking. "Who would have a replicator here?"

"No one," she answered. "That's the point. Your clothes are too perfect. Nothing with our current level of tech would look that pristine."

"Maybe I'm just tidy."

"Besides, you don't even know what Dayla is, do you?"

I stayed silent, jogging along, hoping she'd get bored.

Or angry.

Anything other than that vague amusement and interest.

Or that at least the wind would change, quit teasing me with her scent.

"You know, if you were smart, you'd get some clothes off those guys back there."

I didn't have to look to know she was gesturing towards the pile of corpses we'd left behind us.

"Not really high on my list," I answered. "Besides, I doubt if any of their stuff would fit me."

And it was likely covered with bugs.

And fairly bloody.

"You've got a point there," she conceded. "But still,

you need to do something, or every person you meet is going to want those clothes. The fabric itself would be worth a pile."

Dayla increased her pace and Myria looked down, sizing me up.

It was... uncomfortable.

"Maybe not the boots," she added. "But everything else could be cut down."

Slowly the terrain shifted, more gray-green brush breaking up the rocks, less sand.

"That's the other thing."

God, she wouldn't stop talking.

"Maybe it's different where you're from, but we don't have a whole lot of folks of your size here."

"My whole family is built big," I answered, absently reaching up to scratch Dayla's cheek where she rubbed it against my shoulder.

It was surprisingly soft.

I'd expected it to feel coarse, scratchy.

"That might be the case," Myria continued, "but if you'd quit flirting with Dayla enough to think about it, you'd realize that, whatever you're here for, you're not going to get it, not working alone."

I glared up at her. "What exactly do you know about it," I snapped.

She shrugged. "I don't know anything about what you're doing, but I travel this route pretty often. The first town up ahead is Bitters. Farmers with passes for market day and licensed merchants and bards are the only ones that have the freedom of the gates."

With a click of her tongue, she urged Dayla on, passing me.

"So, if that's where you're going, you may want to think about it. Otherwise, they're going to assume you're an outlaw. And Tewke's men feel pretty strongly about that since the last round of attacks."

Grumbling under my breath, I lengthened my stride till I caught up.

"What do you mean?"

"There's been too much trouble with outlaws, men like those back there." Her voice was tight, strained. "They prey on traders' caravans, make it difficult for goods to travel from one city to the next."

"Hasn't it always been like that? It's not like you're a hub of commerce here."

"Don't be an idiot," she snapped. "We know what the rest of the universe is like. Just because we can't have it doesn't mean we've forgotten."

A hot flush of shame burned my cheeks.

"I'm sorry, that was stupid of me."

"Well, try harder not to be stupid," Myria grumbled. "Are you going to Bitters or not?"

Try not to be stupid.

That wasn't a bad plan.

And whether I wanted her help or not, I clearly could use a guide.

“That’s my first stop, yes.”

“You need a guide, even if you don’t realize it,” she said, smiling as she unrolled a short rope ladder from the side of the oddly shaped saddle.

I swung up behind her on the narrow perch, far too close.

Her scent overwhelmed me, blinding me to everything for a moment, deafening me so I almost lost her next words.

“My rates are cheap.”

Somehow, I doubted that.

MYRIA

"You said merchants, farmers, and musicians," the giant behind me growled.

With that voice, he'd make a fabulous singer.

Pity he didn't seem to be much of a people person.

"I don't see much up here in goods that you're looking to trade," he continued. "And you don't look like a farmer."

"Never can tell," I interrupted him. "I was, once."

"That means you're not anymore."

We moved through the scrubland as the suns rose higher. With luck, we'd be under the shade of the ferum trees soon and could take a break.

"Nope," I sighed, and leaned back to think about the past.

Immediately, I shot forward again.

I'd forgotten he was quite so close behind me.

His broad chest was a comfortable, but somehow unsettling, backrest.

I chattered for a moment to get over the embarrassment. "When an older bard passed through our hamlet ten years ago, I took a chance and apprenticed to him."

For a moment the landscape changed, became the deep greens of my childhood.

"Seems a chancy way out," the stranger commented. "Did you even know the guy?"

"About as well as I know you," I shot back.

And it hadn't mattered. Not really.

Because other than signing up as a foot soldier in one of the warlords' armies, there was no other way off the farm.

And I had to go.

But while I'd always been open, talking to crowds about anything and everything, apparently I felt a little differently talking about my own past.

"Might've been safer to stay home," he muttered, and I could feel him pivot slightly as he scanned the landscape for enemies.

"You might think so, but you'd be wrong."

I thought of my sister, the beauty of the family.

She hadn't been safe at all.

"Tell me about this place we're heading to," he ordered.

"Are you sure? I thought you didn't really need a guide," I couldn't help teasing.

He was just so stuffy.

"Yes, I'm sure. I'm taking your advice to not be stupid."

"Bitters has a proper wall," I started, wondering how much information he really needed. "Tewke does a good job of maintaining it, keeping the infrastructure functioning."

"Another one of your warlords?"

I absently clucked to Dayla. We were getting into enough foliage that she was sure something here must be tasty.

Soon we'd need to stop and get out of the heat.

"Not exactly. He took the city from the previous holder about, oh, five years ago, maybe six. He's held it pretty well ever since."

"Sounds to me like what a warlord would do."

"Trust me on this, he's nothing like the old warlords." I shuddered, remembering my grandmother's stories about the war. "They weren't exactly known for trying to build things up."

I felt him shrug behind me and twisted to turn back towards him. "And while we're on the matter of trust, I really do think you should do something about your clothing as quickly as possible."

He glanced down, obviously reluctant. "I'm not sure

what you think is going to make things less 'off-worlder' but still fit me."

I snorted, turned away. "I'm not the only person who's heard of a ship landing in Lukin, you know."

He sat still as stone.

"Look," I sighed. "Wouldn't it be helpful if you told me what you were actually here for?"

He was rigid and silent.

Finally a murmur, almost a growl.

"Should've sent Geir or Lorcan, dammit. This is their sort of thing. But no, they had to spend time with their mates," he muttered under his breath.

"Look, I'll help you out with the trust thing," I said. "I saw what you did back there, right?"

"What does that have to do with anything?"

I snorted. "I don't know your name, where you're from, or what you're doing here. I do know you could kill me, but still, you're sitting behind me."

I'd been aware of him the entire day, the massiveness of his body. Suddenly, every strong muscle that brushed against me seemed to stand in sharp relief.

"Why did you trust me, then?" he asked, and for the first time, his voice didn't sound abrupt, but actually curious.

I leaned forward to stroke Dayla's neck.

"Dayla seems to like you. And since I've gotten

pretty far on her trusting me, I figured I would trust you, as well."

"Aedan," he grunted after a long moment of silence.

"What?"

"It's my name."

Well, that was a start.

"Alright, Aedan. As soon as we get to that stand of trees, we're going to have to stop for a bit to let Dayla rest and get a snack."

I pushed back the hair that had fallen out of my braid. "And I wouldn't mind getting out of the sun for a while."

I looked longingly at the shade in the distance. I could almost imagine the cool brook that ran through it.

We'd be there soon enough, but I wished I'd stayed in Trandor long enough to earn a few more coins, maybe replaced my old, battered scarves.

Aedan drummed his fingers on his thigh.

But "How long will she need to rest?" was all he asked.

"Not long, and we could use the break, too." I glanced over my shoulder at him. The suns' heat didn't seem to be bothering him in the slightest.

"At least, I do. We'll be in Bitters long before nightfall."

"Once we're there, I'll look for a caravan, something

that's traveling to Lukin. There's no need for you to be involved anymore."

Oh.

"Glad I could get you out of the desert and on your way," I said.

Not really in the mood to talk anymore, I reached for the bag at my side, carefully sliding the retrew out of its carrying case.

"What's that?

I ran my hand down the long neck, checking the strings.

"It's a retrew. It's how I make my living."

I didn't feel like offering up any more information, not if he was being a jerk about things.

I strummed a few chords and adjusted the strings again.

The wild swings of temperature in the desert always wreaked havoc on my tunings.

"What are you doing?"

"Practicing," I answered shortly and started softly singing.

At least he didn't interrupt.

Maybe he was working on that 'don't be an idiot' thing.

By the time we reached the shade, my fingers were limbered up, but I was ready to stop.

We moved into the treeline until Dayla stopped in a

cool glade, surrounded by dark purple shrubs and shaded by the spreading branches far above. Somewhere close I could hear a small stream splashing over rocks.

Perfect.

"You'll have to climb down first," but before the words were fully out of my mouth, he sprung down, not even waiting for the ladder to unroll.

"Well then, that must be handy."

After I climbed down, I unhooked my bow, set it and the retrew carefully to the side, and opened one of the saddlebags.

It was thinner than I would've liked, but I pulled out a loaf of bread. It wasn't nearly as good as it had been fresh.

Hours of traveling under a hot sun had probably served as a second round of baking.

I ripped it in two and handed half to Aedan.

"Sorry, I didn't really have much of a chance to stock up before I left. We can get more food in Bitters."

I checked myself. Well, I would.

He could do whatever the hell he wanted.

He took the bread, tore off a piece, and handed the rest back to me. "I'll be fine until we get to town."

I shrugged, then took a bite of bread and focused on getting Dayla's saddle off.

Every time she was free of the harness, she gave a little shimmy, as if happy to be out of its confines.

I tried to think.

Had she been doing that more often?

"Why did you leave without proper supplies? That doesn't seem to fit in with your whole don't-be-an-idiot plan."

"There was a guy."

I patted Dayla's flank and she headed off deeper into the trees in search of her own meal.

I watched her, hoping she'd come back.

Wouldn't be much to do about it if she didn't.

"What guy?" Aedan persisted.

I took another bite of bread and studied him.

He really always did look angry, didn't he?

"A guy in a tavern. Don't worry about it, I handled things." I stretched out under a tree, glad for its shade. "You're not the only jerk out here, you know?"

Aedan glared, a muscle in his jaw jumping.

"I'm going to check the perimeter. You're far too casual about security."

I listened to the splash of the stream next to us and slipped into a light doze, more than eager to make up for the short night.

Suddenly, a terrified shriek ripped through the quiet glade.

I sprang to my feet, running towards the sound.

Aedan was at my side immediately. "What was that?" he snapped.

"Dayla!" I answered.

We burst from the trees, tearing up the bank of the creek to where Dayla had been grazing.

And a thing from nightmares had caught her.

Sickly gray tendrils flailed, rising from the water, pulling her from the bank into the fast current.

"What the hell is that?" Aedan barked.

"Mardor," I gasped. "But I've never seen one this far south."

"Well, it's here now."

Springing forward, he unsheathed the knife at his side while I raced to Dayla's head.

The razor-sharp claws on her short forearms did her no good as she swiped and thrashed at the mass of tentacles.

"Easy, girl," I crooned. "Steady."

Aedan charged into the water, knife slashing at anything that got in his way.

"Hold her still!" he shouted.

"I'm trying," I snapped, terror making my words harsh.

Dayla was a vegetarian, sure, but that didn't mean she couldn't bite my arm off in her panic.

"It's going to be okay," I promised her, hoping I wasn't lying. "We're working to get you out."

Slowly, her thrashing stopped and she fixed me with a blank gaze.

"That's my girl." I couldn't look away from her, afraid to break whatever daze she was in.

But she was pulled further into the water with a jolt and she began to thrash once more.

"How's it going back there?" I called, deciding that I could learn to play a retrew one-armed if necessary as I reached for her head.

Her talons raked my shoulder, not deep but enough to draw blood.

I gritted my teeth against the pain, and held onto her muzzle, keeping her focus on me.

"Almost," Aedan called out, and with a final splash and squeal from Dayla, the tentacles shuddered and fell limply into the water.

Free, Dayla charged forward, knocking me to the side onto the muddy bank.

I raised myself on one elbow, blinking, then laughed at the sight before me.

"Well, we don't have to worry about your clothes being too noticeable anymore."

Aedan looked at himself and shrugged.

"Not the first time. Not even the first time today."

The fit was still perfect, but you couldn't really tell under the mud and the rips.

His gaze narrowed.

"What happened," he demanded, and before I caught his movement, he was kneeling by my side.

"Dayla just scratched me a bit. She was scared." I brushed away his hands. "It wasn't her fault."

He scowled. "I don't suppose you've got medical supplies in that saddlebag."

"Actually, that is part of my don't-be-an-idiot plan."

I stood up and winced.

The river was brown, muddy from the fight.

"Once the water clears, I wouldn't mind a rinse, as long as that thing is dead."

"I'm good at making things dead," Aedan said. He didn't look like he was joking.

That was…somewhere between comforting and disturbing.

I'd figure it out later.

Except there wasn't going to be a later.

I looked away quickly. "This will stop bleeding soon enough. I'll rinse it, then take care of it. No point in putting a clean bandage over mud."

"You know," Aedan started as we trudged back to where I had left the saddle, to find Dayla happily grazing as if none of the previous minutes of terror had ever happened, "telling me it was a Mardor doesn't help much."

"Yeah, but there wasn't a lot of time for detailed explanations."

I started checking over Dayla, but other than the mud around her haunches, she seemed unharmed.

"One of the reasons the pact outlawed anything hi-tech," I finally continued. "The warlords were making things like that, weapons that couldn't be controlled."

Aedan froze. "That's… a good reason." I guessed wherever he was from didn't have terrors like that.

"When we get to Bitters, I'll have to let them know that one of those monstrosities is so close to town. They'll send a contingent of guards to patrol the riverway, see if anything else is in the area."

After I cleaned off, I gingerly bandaged the cut down my upper arm.

"I can't believe she panicked like that and hurt you. I thought she liked you," Aedan said as I pulled the sleeve of my overshirt back down to cover the bandage.

"And that's the other reason I knew you weren't from around here," I said as I gathered our things together, patted Dayla's side, and moved towards the saddle.

"I'll get that," Aedan interrupted.

I watched as he hefted it over her back as easily as I carried my retrew.

Apparently he had been paying attention, closely too.

As he finished tightening the straps, I continued. "Every kid dreams of finding their own torwynn, riding off, having adventures. It's part of all the songs."

I squeezed another stream of water out of my braid. "You just don't get the chance very often. And not for long. Sure, Dayla likes me well enough," I said, stroking her muzzle, "but she's not really tamed. She's on her own adventure and when she's done, she'll go back to her herd."

He carefully helped me into the saddle, arranged my bags, then swung up behind me.

"Sounds like it'll be lonely."

I clicked, and Dayla headed back to the edge of the trees, striding away towards town.

"Might be. But it's worth it."

AEDAN

By the time we got to Bitters' gates, we were dry, but not exactly looking particularly respectable.

Unlike the desert we'd crossed, the land surrounding the town was green and purple, obviously under cultivation. Not exactly lush, but certainly livable.

Purple, puffy critters that Myria called tessa grazed the low bushes, calling to each other with low, echoing sounds.

The road that had run from the glade where poor Dayla had been attacked by that tentacled thing led to a single point.

An arched opening in a high wall with two pairs of liveried guards inspecting each group of travelers.

Myria had been right.

It didn't look like any single travelers were even trying to get in.

From my perch behind her, I had an unobstructed view of three men and a woman walking behind a cart being pulled by something that was obviously one of Dayla's relatives.

Yellow and pink stripes showed over its back as it lumbered forwards on six stocky legs, and a hard bony ruff protected its neck with spikes running down its snout.

"Not entirely certain how something like that's gonna hide from predators," I muttered, thinking about its slow, heavy movements.

"Zugrin blend in almost perfectly with the grasses in the Pintol swamps," Myria answered under her breath. "But maybe you shouldn't ask any questions until we're sure nobody can overhear and wonder why you don't know the things that everyone does."

Right.

Finally it was our turn to be inspected.

An older man, likely the leader of the guards stationed here, stepped forwards and Dayla shied back.

"Do you have a tag for her?" His face twisted into a scowl, and I tensed just a bit. "All torwynn have to pass inspection before they're allowed access to the city."

"Sure do, hang on a moment," Myria answered.

As if sensing my uneasiness at the situation, she patted my leg once, then moved to dismount.

Despite the bandage, the tang of her blood in the air had haunted my senses for the last three hours.

It was going to take more than a quick pat to get me to settle down.

"Stay put," I grumbled, then leapt down, reaching up to help her.

I might not know what tag she was talking about, but she didn't need to be climbing up and down that flimsy ladder with her arm injured.

She squeezed my hand, then turned to face the guards, a smile bright on her face.

"Sorry about that, banged my arm up a little, it's still sore." A few quick steps and she was between me and the guards.

I didn't like it.

"Here you go." She tapped a thin oval plate that had been riveted to Dayla's harness.

"She was certified city-safe the last time we passed through." A quick scratch of her muzzle, and Dayla huffed her contentment. "She may back up occasionally, but she's no clumsier than most of my dancing partners."

One of the younger guards waggled his eyebrows. "I'm a pretty good dancer, why don't you come try me out?"

My growl must've been louder than I thought because Myria shot me a look, then shooed me to stay behind her.

"I don't know where we're performing tonight, but you can certainly look us up," she said cheerfully.

That wasn't gonna happen.

And who was the guy in the last town that had hassled her so much she'd had to sneak away in the middle of the night?

Surely I'd have enough time to gather the information Vandalar wanted, get his great-aunt, and come back and destroy that asshole.

Just needed a name.

I came back from my pleasant thoughts to catch the end of the conversation.

"…a little tangle with a Mardor back on the riverbank."

"Never been one around here," the older guard scowled. "Not one."

Myria put her hands on her hips.

"Doesn't mean there can't be one now," she snapped. "And what happens when it comes up closer to the farms and drags some poor little tessa into the water? Or a farmer's child? Who is going to be responsible for that?"

She held his gaze and finally, the guard backed down.

"Fine, I'll see that it's reported."

"My thanks." She grabbed Dayla's harness and started walking through the gate.

The guards stepped forward to block my way. "You're authorized to enter, but he's not."

"What? He's my apprentice."

All four of the guards stared at me, probably trying to imagine me with one of those little instruments in my hand.

I didn't blame them. I'd probably crush it before coaxing a tune from the thing.

I hunched down, tried to look smaller.

I don't think it worked.

"Fine," Myria sashayed back through the guards to my side. "We weren't going to tell anyone yet, because it's terrible for my act, but we've just gotten married."

And with that, she leaned forward on her toes and twined her arms around my neck.

Her lips brushed mine.

"Sorry about this," she whispered.

Then she kissed me.

And there was nothing for her to be sorry for.

I pulled her closer to me, lifting her from the ground, desperate for more of the sweet taste of her.

Her lips parted as she gasped and my tongue plundered her mouth, twining with her own as her fingers somehow worked through my hair.

And everything was lost.

The mission, the Empire, all of it vanished into that one point.

The soft, clever woman in my arms.

The guard's whistle broke through the moment, and I let her down gently so that I could quickly kill the asshole.

"Honey, that's enough," Myria said, cheeks flaming as she grabbed my arm.

Not looking at the guards, I lifted her into the saddle and swung up behind her.

With the click of Myria's tongue, Dayla moved through the gate and this time, no one stopped us, just handed up a piece of paper.

"Don't lose your entry document," the older guard said. "Either you, or your husband."

"Sorry about that," she said when we were out of earshot. "I guess I got carried away and--"

"Where are we heading?" I cut her off.

She wasn't the only one who'd gotten carried away.

I didn't want to think about it.

Not now.

"Right." A woman pushing a handcart cut us off, and Myria bent forward to stroke Dayla's neck.

I muffled a groan

She'd been doing that all afternoon and every time, it pushed the lush curves of her ass tight against me.

Maybe she couldn't tell through those coarsely woven leggings that she wore, but if she kept it up, it would be impossible to hide the results.

She coaxed Dayla through the surprisingly busy traffic, carts pulled by zugrin and their relatives, push-carts with produce and goods of all kinds, a few torwynn and their riders.

"The market isn't for a few days yet," Myria commented. "We should still be able to get a room at the Fox and Cub, unless somebody else has already taken up residence. They'll be happy to have some entertainment."

I didn't say anything, busy watching the crowded streets.

Watching her.

She confidently guided Dayla through smaller streets until she found a tall, half-timbered building with a swinging sign out front.

The sign displayed a spotted beast of some kind leaning against a tree.

"You can't tell me that whatever the Void that creature is called is perfectly camouflaged in its native habitat," I said as I lifted her down.

"I really can get off and on by myself," she muttered. Then Dayla nuzzled Myria's wounded arm and she winced. "Probably." Glancing at the sign, a wicked grin lit her face. "And yes, actually, I could tell you about that 'creature', as you call it. But I won't, so you'll just have to wonder where such a place would be."

Leading Dayla to the back of the building, she gave instructions for her care and feeding, then together we went inside the inn.

A tall man with burly arms was lifting a table, while another who might have been his twin, scrubbed the exposed floor.

"Brom! Edrel!" Myria called out. "Are you working your way out of trouble, or earning up points for a favor with the old man?"

With a booming laugh, the floor scrubber tossed down his mop and picked up Myria, swinging her around.

It was harder than it should have been to stay still and let him touch her.

"Look who's here, Dad," he shouted to the back of the room. "Myria, my love!" an elderly man with a shock of salt and pepper hair sticking out from his head like a slightly tarnished halo emerged.

Once he came out from the bar, I could see that his odd gait was from where he leaned heavily on a crutch, swinging it with every step.

"I thought it was about time for you to make your way to us, but I expected you closer to market day."

Myria tossed her head. "I couldn't wait a moment longer to see you, Narvin." She smiled up at me and batted her eyelashes outrageously. "But you might have to share my affections."

Sharp eyes turned to me. "And who's this, then?"

A pause.

We could say anything.

But if someone checked that document...

"Well," Myria started, "a lot's happened since I was through last time." She tucked her arm into mine. "He's my husband, Aedan."

"Oh, lovely, lovely, lovely," the old man crowed, then his eyes narrowed. "But he's not taking very good care of you, not like a mate should."

Brom and Edrel turned towards me, expressions carefully blank.

"Narvin!" Myria's outraged voice rang through the room. "He's fine!"

"If that's the case, how'd you get hurt? I can see the edge of a bandage poking out from your sleeve clear across the room, girl."

"Even as big as he is," Myria admitted, "he can't be on both sides of Dayla at the same time." Her face sobered. "There was a Mardor. It tried to drag Dayla in. He saved us."

"Well, I'll get the word out, then," Narvin said. "Make sure folks keep watch."

"We already told the guards," I said, not really

wanting the old man and his sons to be any further involved in our affairs than they already seemed to be.

He snorted. "Like they're going to do anything. Trust me, I can get the word out a lot more efficiently than those buffoons."

Narvin turned, more agile on the crutch that I would have expected. "Boy!" he shouted to the back of the room.

"Come get singer Myria's bags, take them upstairs to the third room, in the back. Nice and quiet. Let you rest." He grinned wickedly. "If rest is what you're after."

Blushing, Myria stepped away from me. "So while we're here, I was thinking about changing my set. Let me know what you think."

While the two of them talked, I slipped outside to get a better feel of the town.

From up on Dayla's back, it had been too hard to get a sense of what was going on.

Men and women passed by, most of them looking tough.

Tired.

I wandered out into the larger street, watching the foot traffic. Tidy whitewashed buildings were mixed with those made of stone.

Muddy streets brought a low level of grime to everything, despite obvious attempts to keep things clean.

Couldn't be avoided.

No one would ever call me Vandalar's biggest fan. But maybe I could convince him to get here sooner rather than later.

It wasn't right that this planet had been abandoned like this.

And then I remembered the look on Myria's face when she talked about the monsters that had been created in the war.

What would she think if she realized her traveling companion, her 'husband', was kindred to it, both in design and purpose.

I snorted. At least not in appearance.

That would make it hard to do the job.

I scouted a little further, down a block and then another, watching.

In the hustle and bustle of merchants getting ready for the market, this might be a good time to leave, find another traveler, or head out on my own.

Surely not every town was so tightly guarded.

Something twisted in my gut.

It insisted that the practical decision would be to stay with Myria.

She had the perfect opportunity to travel, to talk to people, to get the information I needed.

I'd be smart to stay with her, have her tell me more

about the situation on the planet, make sure I was prepared to deal with Flame.

But I could still taste her on my lips.

Smart or not, I had to stay away from her.

I searched through the streets, marked a couple likely looking places to meet up with another caravan, then headed back to the inn.

Even if I was leaving, I wouldn't do it without saying goodbye.

I might be a jerk, but Doc had insisted that we had some manners.

I headed upstairs, following her scent.

If the old man hadn't already made her change that bandage, I was going to insist on it before I left.

Who knew what sort of infection she could pick up from the mud she'd fallen in?

And then to rinse it in a stream.

An open stream with who knew what swimming in it.

Madness.

Working myself up to images of gangrene, I flung open the door to the room. "Don't tell me they don't even have healing wands on this --"

I froze, mouth agape.

Myria sat in a hip bath, eyes wide as she looked over her shoulder at me.

All I could see was the smooth line of her back through the steam.

"Well, come in and close the door," she hissed. "We're supposed to be married, right? You've seen it all before."

There was nothing to say to that.

There were lots of things I wanted to say to that.

But I didn't.

I stepped into the room and closed the door behind me, then carefully looked away.

Void.

Who put a mirror there?

I turned again, searching for something safe to look at.

"So, what's the plan?" I asked, voice perfectly normal.

Perfectly.

She splashed as she scrubbed.

"I'm going to play for the evening, hopefully picking up enough coins and information to make it all worthwhile. I'll stay through the market fair, unless..."

She trailed off. "What's your plan?" she asked quietly.

What was my plan?

Thinking, I caught another glimpse of her back in the mirror.

She was too thin, but her lean curves were still beautiful, still called to me.

I thought about someone in this town hassling her, driving her away before she earned enough coin, ate enough food.

Rage washed through me, but then a cold voice from the back of my mind answered.

What are you going to do about it?

You're going to leave, now or later.

True.

But.

I already knew her.

Already trusted her.

"How do you feel about leaving sooner than that?"

MYRIA

That was unexpected.

I stepped out of the tub onto the thick woven mat and dried myself off, thinking quickly.

"I need to perform at least one night, or my reputation will be ruined," I mused aloud. "Running out on one engagement was bad enough. Trandor is a small village, and everybody knew what was going on. Here...I just can't do that to Narvin."

I snorted and reached for my clothes. "Besides, we'll need the coin."

"Don't worry about that," Aedan interrupted. "This is my trip, you're my guide. I'll buy the supplies, and I should be paying you."

I turned to study his broad back, still carefully

turned away from me. I found myself admiring the strong lines, the pride.

"As long as you're clear that my guiding you is all you're paying me for."

I still remembered that kiss at the gate.

How his lips had burned against mine, how his hands pulled me to him, claiming, possessing.

How much I'd liked it.

"Of course."

"The water's still hot," I said, pulling on my dirty clothes with regret.

He shook his head. "I'll get one later."

"No," I said, wearily finger-combing my hair. "You're not going to ask them to boil enough water for a second bath. It's not that easy here. You've got to remember that."

A stricken look passed over his face. "Right."

After checking the street for the orange and black tabards of Flame's men, I breathed easier and went down the stairs while Aedan bathed.

Relaxed, I wandered to the small courtyard behind the inn and fed some long blue leaves to Dayla.

The boy, one of Narvin's numerous grandchildren, had done a good job with the torwynn, putting her in a dry, roomy pen with plenty of branches within easy reach.

She still preferred to be hand-fed.

Dayla huffed contentedly, laying her head over my shoulder, pulling me in for the torwynn equivalent of a hug.

"Doesn't look like anyone followed us, but still, rest quickly," I murmured to her. "I think it's going to be an adventure for us both."

By the time my hair was dry, Aedan was downstairs, looking for me.

"Come on," I said. "We've got some time before the inn fills up and makes it busy enough to be worth putting on a show."

"Time for what?"

"Time to hit the market. There will be enough vendors set up by now that we can get what we need for a trip."

As we stepped into the street, I slid my hand into the crook of his elbow and fought down the urge to look around.

If anyone was still looking for me, it was as a lone bard, not part of a couple.

Aedan looked down at our entwined arms, surprised.

"Newlyweds? Remember?"

"Of course." He flushed, dark under the tan skin, and I thought about how his eyes had looked when he walked in on me in the bath.

And then pushed that away, quickly.

Back to the practicalities.

"I assume we're going all the way to Lukin?" I asked as we reached the edge of the market, rows of brightly covered booths stretched out before us, filling the entire town square.

"Yes. And without too much delay ,if possible," he added.

"Any reason?"

"There is a timing issue." Aedan looked more serious than usual. "I calculated everything before I--"

I kicked his ankle, just a bit, and he blinked. "We should be fine. But delays should be kept to a minimum."

Something about his tone made me nervous.

"We'll still need clothing for you," I decided. "I'll wash mine out tonight, and they'll dry by morning. We'll rinse yours as well, but if possible, I'd like to find a jacket, a cloak, something that might mask your size just a bit."

I looked up at his bulk and sighed.

"Or maybe we should just look for fabric. I can stitch something up as we ride, have it ready before we arrive."

"That seems like a lot of trouble," he argued.

"Think of it as part of the service," I teased, bumping his hip with mine. "Besides, it's very wifely."

We headed straight to the garment quarter, but despite my precautions, the back of my neck itched.

I still couldn't see anyone following us.

Probably I was just jumpy after the last few days.

I turned my mind to shopping.

I'd rather acquire travel provisions when we were closer to leaving.

No reason to let anyone think we were heading out before the fair ended, no reason to have anyone speculating.

We stopped at the first stall and I couldn't help the little squeal of delight that escaped my lips.

Lovely fabrics, cunningly woven, thoughtfully designed, stirred something in my heart.

I enjoyed music, sure, could sing and play well enough.

It served a purpose.

Gave me my freedom.

But if I had a true love, it would be for beautiful fabrics, elegant clothing.

It was a useful skill, being able to read the hidden clues about a person by the cut and quality of their clothing.

That skill was what had made Aedan's origins so obvious.

But I'd never be able to afford any of the lovely things here.

"Wait," I paused, caught by a bright riot of color. Flowers of purple and yellow bloomed on a blue background, the colors blending and blurring together.

"I want to see that one."

The shopkeeper looked at me, at my ragged, dirty clothing. "Let's see the color of your coin before you ruin such a fine piece of fabric with your hands."

Aedan loomed behind me.

"Excuse me?" Menace threaded the words, and the vendor swallowed.

"No offense, a man's got to look after his goods."

He didn't bring up money again, but gently eased the fabric from where it had been neatly folded between other pieces of cloth.

"Your lady's got a good eye," he commented, stretching the thin piece out across the top of the other fabrics.

"It's just a scrap, really," he added, "but I don't know when I've last seen something so fine."

No need to touch it, although my fingers were itching to stroke its silky sheen.

I could see the quality from where I stood.

Knew where it must've come from.

"Aedan," I started, but didn't need to continue.

"We'll take it," he said bluntly. "How much?"

As we wandered away from the booth, I carefully

draped the fabric around my neck. If anything, it made my clothes look even shabbier in contrast.

And I didn't care in the slightest.

"You need to learn to bargain a little," I said. "But thank you."

"You wanted it," was his only response.

I squeezed his hand. "I want a lot of beautiful things, but I don't have to have them all. This one I wanted because it's like you."

"What?"

I held the fabric up, so fine I could clearly see the other shops through it, the colors so vibrant that they tinted everything.

"It's not from here."

I ran the end of the scarf through my fingers. "And I suspect whatever you're here for, it involves a lady."

That telltale muscle in his jaw twitched.

"You're the one that keeps reminding me I shouldn't talk about things in public places." He looked down, touched the scarf softly. "But it's not surprising to find this here. A little worrying, perhaps."

"Should we ask the merchant where he got it?" I asked. "He might be able to help you trace it."

He thought for a moment, then shook his head. "No. I'm pretty sure we know where she is. I don't want to call attention to us yet." Aedan looked into the distance, at something I couldn't see. "But I think I might need to hurry a bit more."

Not worrying, not at all.

"Well then, let's go find some more options. I don't think I'll be dressing you in brocades anytime soon."

He scowled, and I let my imagination play, just for a moment.

He'd be handsome, if I could ever talk him into clothing that didn't look completely utilitarian.

He'd be handsome, if I could talk him out of his clothing, too, an evil voice whispered, and I pulled my new scarf up to hide my burning cheeks.

One row away I found a merchant with a wide variety of much more practical fabrics.

While I was browsing, Aedan waited for the woman to step away. "What are the different fabrics made from, can you tell?"

"That's a safe enough thing to ask," I whispered back. "Most people don't pay that much attention."

"This," I pointed to a bolt of coarse gray fabric, "is from the leaves of the desil tree. These are softer, but not quite as strong." I gestured to another stack of brightly colored clothes. "Soto branches peel their bark in layers, and when it's pulped it takes a dye beautifully."

"Oh!" I grabbed a bolt of bright blue fabric and held it up to his face. "This would match your eyes-"

I stopped. It did match his eyes, brought them out into startling, bright sapphire fires.

Aedan's size and breadth were unusual, but not unheard of.

But his eyes, his eyes were wild, feral.

For a moment, he didn't seem exactly human.

I staggered back, startled.

Aedan caught me, his hands grabbing my upper arms, but still careful of my bandage.

"Never mind, not your color after all."

I started flipping through fabrics, looking for other options, trying to clear my mind of that piercing stare.

"Why don't we just get some of that stuff?" Aedan pointed to the coarser material. "You said it's tough, right?"

"It's also tough to sew." And not at all pleasant to work with.

I kept looking over the bolts, passing over a lovely gray, afraid that even the slightest cast of blue would bring too much attention to his eyes.

Whatever his secrets were, I didn't want to accidentally reveal them.

I had secrets of my own to protect.

"How's this?" I held up a nice rich brown, completely forgettable, but not unpleasant.

The woman came over, knowing with the extra

sense that all good merchants have that a sale was ready to happen.

"We'll take…" I eyed Aedan, figuring out how much fabric we'd need. Something that would flow and move with him as he fought, something that wouldn't constrict or bind him.

"All of it," he said. "Let's start there."

That would do it.

"And do you have a shirt, a..." he waved at my torso, "something in her size?" he asked the woman.

"What? We're not shopping for me, remember?"

His lips twisted into a half grin. "You'll make better coin when you perform tonight if you have something clean."

Which was true. But I didn't have to admit it.

Even if I did love the long tunic we decided on, the color of smoke, with russet bands at the cuffs.

We packed it up with his plain brown material and the various sundries I'd need to finish the jacket, and headed back to the inn.

"Dammit," I muttered.

Somehow, it'd gotten later than I thought, and the streets were already darkening. If I didn't get back to Narvin's soon, there was a chance some other bard would poach my spot.

"Let's cut through here," I suggested on impulse, pointing out a narrow alley.

"Are you certain?" Aedan asked.

"Sure," I nodded. Mostly sure, at least. "The guards patrol pretty frequently, especially when it's close to market time. It'll be fine."

Halfway through the alley, Aedan stiffened.

"By any chance, are you armed?" he asked softly.

"Nothing on me," I answered as quietly as I could. "Just my bow, back in my room. I don't usually need weapons to go shopping."

"Someone's behind us," Aedan said. "Just out of sight."

I couldn't hear anything, but right then, I felt comfortable trusting his instincts.

"Do you think we can get out of here before they reach us?" I asked, nerves suddenly tight.

"Not without running into the guys in front of us," he said dryly. "And if possible, I'd rather not lead them back to the inn."

"Unless they already know where we're staying," I threw in.

"Well, you're cheerful." He rubbed the back of his neck. "Void. How did they even find me?" I shrugged, my stomach tight. "I did say you stood out some, but this seems a little excessive." I pivoted to watch the shadows, look for anything that might be to our advantage.

"Maybe they were watching to see who came after

that scarf," he mused.

"Seems like a long shot, but does it really matter right now?"

"Not really. Here."

He handed me the knife strapped to his belt.

In his hands, it looked more like a dagger. In mine, it was closer to a short sword.

"Tell me you know how to use that."

"I can manage," I answered. "But won't you need it?"

He flashed a grin, the first real smile I'd seen on his face. "No. I'll be fine."

A thought struck, and I scowled. "Dammit."

"What's wrong?" he said sharply.

"The fabric. It's going to get ruined."

Now even I could hear footsteps approaching from both ends of the alley as the shadows were getting deeper.

He turned and looked at me, amused.

"You're worried about your fabric."

"And the sewing supplies," I argued. "You have no idea how hard it is to get needles some days." My shoulders slumped. "And I liked my new tunic."

He snorted softly. "Give it here."

I handed over the parcel and, with a quick jump, he clung halfway up the wall of the building that closed us into the alley, holding on with one hand to a ledge I could barely make out in the growing gloom.

“That will have to do.” He tucked the parcel out of sight, then dropped down silently next to me. “There’s a nook in the wall, try to stay in it as much as possible. I’ll be back as soon as I can.”

“Wait!” I called.

Our unwanted company was finally close enough to see clearly.

Four burly men in torn, dirty leathers approached from the direction we’d been heading, three more from behind.

They were close, but I needed just one moment.

Aedan paused next to me, confused by my demand.

I reached up and kissed him lightly.

“Be safe.”

With a wicked grin, he sprang away into battle, and I braced to defend myself.

AEDAN

I'd spent my life fighting. Planned to go on that way.

And it had never been so hard to go into battle knowing that Myria was behind me.

I gauged the quartet of attackers as they approached.

Big and tough, but they moved heavily.

All carried daggers, with short metal clubs clutched in their other hand.

Not a bad idea, they would work to block a blade or could strike a lethal blow. Not as unwieldy as a shield and better for close-up work than a full-sized staff.

Easier to hide than a sword.

But still, they were only human.

I glanced back down the alley, gauging the leader of the three approaching us and taking in their stances, their skill.

"Stay back as long as you can," I told Myria, "let me handle it."

Not that I expected her to, but I had to have a little hope.

The narrow confines of the alley were to our advantage. They couldn't get two abreast, couldn't mob and overwhelm us.

"Think you could speed it up? The lady's got places to be."

I waited for them to get closer, listening until I heard the footfalls behind me.

I could have charged them, swooping through their line and back again before they could regroup.

But that would have left Myria too exposed, undefended.

So I waited.

"Think you're a funny one," came a hoarse shout from not far behind me.

Close enough.

Leaping up, I caught the ledge where I'd stashed Myria's fabric, then kicked off, launching myself into the group of three.

I blocked the blow of a metal club with my forearm, twisted around, and broke my opponent's wrist. Then I smashed his head into the brick wall.

One.

Dropping to a low crouch, I swept out with one foot and knocked the legs out from under the next attacker.

He fell badly, and it was the work of an instant to snap his neck while he was still stunned.

Two.

Grabbing the knife and club that the second man had carried, I sprang at the third, blocking a low thrust to my belly while dragging my borrowed blade across his throat.

Three.

I dashed back up the alley.

It had only taken a moment, but that meant the second party of attackers were that much closer to Myria.

"What the hell kind of monster are you?" one of them shouted as blood from his friend's severed jugular artery gushed over him.

Four.

"An impatient one," I growled.

But there wasn't time for much more conversation with that one. Fear made him clumsy, his thrusts sloppy, without much force at all.

Five.

The next one actually had some skill.

Killing him took more than a minute, almost two.

Six.

I spun, searching. Where was…

Oh, Void, no.

Seven had found Myria.

She defended herself well, but he was easily twice her size.

With a roar I sprang forward, tackling him away from her.

He was dead before he hit the ground.

"Are you all right?" I demanded as Myria stared around her with wide eyes. "Did he hurt you?"

She shook her head slowly, still not blinking.

"He hit me once with the club," her whispered words barely breaking the silence, "but I don't think any ribs are broken."

She rubbed her side, grimacing. "It's going to be a hell of a bruise, though."

Slowly, I realized her shock wasn't from fighting with her attacker.

"Are you afraid of me?" I asked quietly.

She took a shaky breath, then another.

"No. If you'd wanted to kill me, you could've done that out in the desert, left my body, taken Dayla." She shook her head slowly. "But, no one moves like that. You've got to be more careful."

My muscles relaxed at her words.

Attackers with blades and clubs were one thing.

I wasn't ready for this other, murkier battle.

"I know we're running late," I said dryly. "But are you all right for a minute more? I want to see who those jokers are."

She nodded and moved forward.

"What are you doing?" I snapped.

"As your guide, I'd like to ask if you have any idea what any of the local clans' colors are. Do you?"

I glared at her. "No."

"And do you know what any of the tattoos mean?"

"No."

Apparently, there was even more information I'd be bringing back to Vandalar.

"Then, if we're going to get back to Narvin's on time, you need to let me help." She tapped her foot. "Come on, it's not like it's the first time I've seen a body."

But our quick search didn't turn anything up.

No colors that she recognized, no tattoos, no jewelry, no marks.

Nothing.

"Maybe we should have kept the last one alive, questioned him," she said.

"He got a blow in on you," I answered as I led her out of the alley, senses stretched as far as possible for any further incidents. "It's not like he was gonna live."

"You're sweet, in a completely terrifying way, do you know that?"

I stared down at her.

"No one, not even my brothers' mates, has ever called me sweet."

"You have brothers?"

"Yeah."

She didn't ask any more questions and I didn't offer any more answers, just retrieved the parcel and, with one arm around her shoulders, hurried her back to the inn.

But her mood quickly quieted as we approached the inn.

"There you are!" Narvin said, swinging across the crowded room towards us.

When we left, it had been fairly empty. Now you could tell that market time was approaching. Men and women of all ages crowded in, shouting for drinks.

Several people, all looking vaguely like Narvin, scurried back and forth between tables, fetching food and drinks, all smiling.

"Told you we've have a crowd tonight!"

"I'll just run upstairs and get changed real quick," Myria said. "Sorry that we're late."

"Pah!" Narvin said. "Let 'em wait, get their appetite up. I'll send one of the boys up with your supper."

He gave a broad, toothless grin. "I've been telling everyone what a treat they're in for, even sent out some of the boys across town to bring in the merchants."

"Great," Myria said, rolling her eyes. "Let's hope I can live up to whatever they've promised."

"Nonsense," the old man argued. "You're always the best singer that comes through." He looked thoughtful. "Well, these days…"

"Quick," Myria stage-whispered, a warm smile of her own for Narvin. "Dinner will get cold if he starts telling us about the old days, with their better singers, and much more interesting songs."

I fell in behind her as we climbed the stairs.

What an odd place. They were missing so much of the basic comforts of civilization. And they knew it.

But still they found the energy to make lives, make things of beauty, friends, families.

Even if they were stuck on a ball of mud.

While we waited for dinner to come up, Myria unrolled the length of fabric, held a section against my shoulders and another against my back from neck to knees, then began deftly cutting.

"How do you know what to do?" I asked, watching her sure movements.

"I can just see it, what needs to be done," she answered, mouth full of pins as she cut.

It seemed like a sort of sorcery, taking a flat piece of fabric, and with such basic tools, turning it into a three-dimensional object.

Then again, I wasn't completely sure how the replicators worked either.

Maybe it was all sorcery.

Dinner came in the form of hot lentil cakes served with an assortment of sauces, all remarkably spicy.

"They let your sister back in the kitchen?" Myria asked the boy as he returned with clay goblets of water. "No one else's food has quite such a kick."

The boy grinned, blushing, and backed out without answering.

"Someone's got a crush on you," I commented.

"Unlucky for him that I'm a married woman," she said.

Finishing dinner quickly, she shook out the new tunic on the bed.

"It's nice to have something new," she said softly, running her fingers over the reddish bits at the cuffs.

I hadn't really thought about how she made her living.

Constantly traveling, never putting down roots. Didn't she miss her family?

"I guess always being on the move means you don't get much shopping time," I teased.

"It has other compensations." A smile lightened her face, but for a moment, it had been tinged with sadness.

Myria shook out her hair and reached for the hem of her dirty tunic.

I turned away quickly, but swung back when she hissed in pain.

"I hate to ask," she said, "but I'm going to need a hand."

"What?" I blurted.

"I can't pull it off over my head without pulling at the bruised area."

I went to her side, trying to look away while pulling the dirty tunic off and sliding the new one over her shoulders.

But I couldn't help catching glimpses of her body. It was lean and lightly muscled from a life on the road, her deep golden skin marred by the already coloring bruise on her side.

Luckily the new tunic opened all the way down the front, and once I helped her pull it over her shoulders, she sighed in relief.

"That'll do it."

"Button that thing up, then let me see your side."

"It's fine," she argued, but once the front of her shirt was fastened, she lifted the hem high enough for me to examine the mark across her ribs.

"May I?"

She nodded, sharp white teeth biting on her lower lip.

I carefully ran my hands over her injured side, her skin softer than anything I'd ever touched. Palpating her ribs as lightly as I could, I stopped at her wince of pain.

"I don't think anything's cracked," I sighed. "But without better instruments, I don't know for certain."

Her wide amber eyes met mine and we both froze for a moment. Leaning towards each other, my hand skimmed across her belly to pull her closer…

She pulled away, tugging her shirt down, and grabbed the carrying case for her retrew.

"Come on, we shouldn't be any later." She carefully wrapped the scarf around her neck, pulling her hair loose to cascade down her back. "This is the fun part."

We'd see about that.

The inn might've been full before, but as we descended the stairs, I found it was packed now.

Myria sauntered through the crowd, and people drew back respectfully, staying out of her way.

My tension levels dropped, just a little bit.

Maybe what she had said was true.

Maybe her position as a bard, bringer of news from

town to town as well as the local entertainment, really did make her safe.

At least, safer.

Maybe.

Still, I made my way to the side of the room, placing my back against the wall so that I could see her and keep an eye on the crowd.

One of Narvin's family came up and handed her a tall mug of something that she quaffed down with obvious glee.

When she lowered it with a thunk back onto the bar, the crowd cheered.

"All right," she called out. "Who's ready for the tale of Kenji?"

Apparently, they all were, from the shouting.

I settled back to listen to the story, the improbable adventures of a soldier during the civil war.

The battle scenes sounded like nonsense, but apparently he'd done enough good to be remembered.

More than half the crowd sang along with the chorus.

A popular hero.

The same boy that had brought Myria her drink came up to my side. "Can I bring you anything?" he was barely audible over the noise of the room.

Void.

Whatever I ordered, I'd likely put my foot in it.

Something else that should have been in the mission notes.

"I'll take whatever she's having," I finally decided. That should be safe enough.

"Hot water with a little bit of citri juice?" He was confused for a moment, then shrugged. "Whatever you'd like."

No, that wasn't what I'd like.

But apparently it was what I was going to get.

As the evening wore on, I watched Myria work the crowd, seamlessly moving from war ballads to rowdy drinking songs, with a few slower instrumental pieces to rest her throat.

"And now for the news," she called out, loudly strumming discordantly to get the crowd's attention.

Myria glanced my way, and for a moment, I stiffened.

She knew something had landed in Lukin.

Would that be part of the news?

Would we have other adventurers vying to find out what had arrived, broking the ban of Kerrind's exile?

And then she began a singsong chant, clearly composed and memorized during the long hours of travel on Dayla's back.

"In Trandor town, farmer Spand has a bumper crop of jemi, seeking extra hands to bring it in before the fair,

"The Lord of Grandoth is ailing, seeking his lost heir,

"Heavy rains in the north mountains washed out the bridge, travelers beware."

On and on she went, the small news in the large, and everyone paid attention.

No one knew what would be of use to them, what would make a difference in their lives.

I listened just as intently.

But she spoke nothing of the landing of a spaceship.

Finally, she stopped and one by one voices from the crowd called out.

More pieces of news, more bits of information for her to carry on to the next town and the next.

"I'll tell you something you should know," a slurred voice shouted from the back of the room. "You're not nearly as clever as you think."

A dark man in an orange and black tabard shoved his way through the crowd.

Myria rolled her eyes, turning to carefully place her retrew in its carrying case.

"I never said I was clever, Kaljak," she said softly. "I said I wasn't interested."

So that was the reason she'd been driven from the last town.

He reached for her and, in a moment, I was at her side.

"I don't think so, buddy," I snapped. "Keep it up, and we'll move it outside."

Red tinted my vision.

It would've been vastly satisfying to tear this smarmy jackass into a bloodied pulp where he stood, but Myria seemed fond of Narvin.

It wouldn't do to mess up his inn.

Myria placed her hand on the small of my back, rubbing in small soothing circles until the mindless rage receded.

A little bit.

"Honey, I know we don't want any trouble with one of Flame's captains."

Her voice didn't put any extra stress on the last two words, but her fingers switched from their soothing movements to sharp taps on my skin.

Flame's captain.

Interesting, I thought.

Either the uniforms had been designed by someone who was colorblind, or someone who wanted to make damn sure his troops were recognized at all times.

This was the first concrete bit of information I had about the warlord. And it was somewhat revealing.

Who would promote a lout like this?

Only another lout, probably.

I didn't have long to think about the possibilities.

"Damn straight you don't," the newcomer said, lurching to the side to make another grab for Myria.

She stood her ground. "I really don't think you should do that," she commented mildly.

At that moment, two options sprang to my mind.

Obviously, just killing the guy was first.

But her closeness gave me pause. And then a second, just as agreeable notion, arose.

"Stop harassing my wife," I said, loud enough for the crowd to hear. "Is this the way Flame treats bards? Or does he have no respect for anyone?"

An ugly murmur rippled through the crowd and I turned my back to Kaljak for a much pleasanter view.

I slipped my arms around Myria's waist and pulled her to me.

"I'm not sorry about this at all," I said, then lifted her to my lips. Her fingers twined in my hair as she turned her face up to meet mine.

The fire, the connection I'd felt at the gate, it hadn't been a fluke.

The taste of her, the feel of her wrapped in my arms was right.

Perfect.

But before I could fall completely under her spell, a hand fell on my shoulder.

"I claimed that whore first," Kaljak snarled.

Well then.

Apparently he really was an idiot.

I carefully lowered Myria back to the floor, smoothed her hair back from her cheek, and turned.

Brom and Edrel had parted the crowd, crude cudgels clenched in their hands as they prepared to take on the offender.

"Thanks," I said to Brom. "You may want to step back a bit, though."

His eyebrows shot up, then he grinned.

Arms spread wide to hold the crowd back, he and his brother made an opening in the room for me.

And without another word, I decked Kaljak, fancy tabard or not.

He sprawled on the floor, a thin trail of blood streaming from his nose.

"That's enough," Myria said softly. "We don't want to bring trouble to these people."

I turned back to her. "Not planning to, but no one is hassling my wife."

I picked her up again and this time when our lips met, I bent forward, devouring her, desperate for her taste, for her touch.

She broke away, panting.

"I think we ought to move the show upstairs," she said, and with a whoop, I swept her into my arms.

The men and women gathered in the room cheered

as Narvin's sons dragged the unconscious Kaljak outside.

"Alright, you bums." Narvin shouted to the crowd. "The newlyweds have other things to do. I know at least some of you can keep a decent tune."

As we ascended the stairs, Narvin called up behind us. "And I don't want to see you until breakfast!"

MYRIA

I had no idea how we got to the room. My entire body was on fire, every fiber burning for his touch.

But here we were, the door closed behind us.

Aedan sat on the bed, with me still cradled in his arms.

With a delicacy I hadn't imagined he possessed, he stroked the hair back from my face and cupped my cheek.

"Are you sure about this?" he asked gruffly. "We can stop now, no one's watching."

A cold shiver of humiliation gripped me and I pushed away.

"Were you just doing that to get me away from Kaljak?" I scrambled back further, trying to get to my feet.

"What? No!" he insisted. "Not at all. I was doing that because I wanted to." His voice dropped lower. "Because I needed to." He scrubbed a hand over his face. "And to be honest, me kissing you was probably the only thing that kept that jerk alive."

Oh. That was flattering.

And scary.

"Still, I need to know," he repeated. "Are you sure? About this? About me?"

Was I sure?

There were things I didn't know about him, I was sure about that.

Big things. Important things.

Maybe things I wasn't ready to know.

But I was already sure about so many things about him.

How he was so careful with his strength. How protective he was.

How he'd delighted in finding a gift for me, just because I'd admired it.

"Let me answer you," I said, and walked back into the circle of his arms.

He kissed me until I was breathless, my body prickling at every touch.

Like I was the finest crystal, he laid me on the bed and slowly rained kisses down my throat, across the curve of my collarbone.

Beginning to unbutton my tunic, he spread it open to expose my breasts inch by inch, driving me wild with his agonizing slowness.

He laid a trail of kisses around and between my breasts, then back up to nip and lick at one tightened nipple, while he finished unbuttoning the tunic with the other hand.

I ran my hands through his hair, so soft and fine, as I arched beneath his touch.

"Hold still," he murmured against my skin, and continued to kiss a path back down to my waistband.

At his unspoken urging, I lifted my hips, and he slid off my pants and low boots in quick, smooth motions.

"Of all the things I have seen on this planet, or any other," he said, gazing down on me, eyes dark with hunger, "I've never wanted anything, anyone, like you."

"I'm not sure that's much of a compliment to the rest of your Empire," I said, but any other words were lost as he knelt between my legs, raising my knees until my feet rested on his shoulders.

Before my next breath, he began his delicate assault on the soft flesh of my inner thighs.

Teasing, taunting, he alternated kissing and licking until I could've screamed with frustration.

"Please," I begged, lost to all shame.

Finally he turned his attention to my dripping folds,

and at the first thrust of his tongue against me, I shattered.

When I caught hold of my senses again, I found myself pressed against his bare chest, one strong arm holding me tightly against him.

His other hand fell between my thighs, stroking, coaxing the wave of sensations to build and swell.

"You're the one that's sweet," he murmured into my hair as his fingers slid through my slick folds.

"Aedan!" I cried against his chest as one thick finger slowly penetrated me.

"Sweet to taste," he said, his hand continuing its slow rock, in and out, deeper each time.

My breaths came in shuddering gasps.

"Sweet to hear," and he slid a second finger in me, filling me, pushing me closer to the edge.

"Sweet to touch." His hand twisted, pressing against my aching clit.

I thrashed against him as I came undone again, held tightly in his strong grip, blind and deaf to anything but his touch and him calling my name.

I WOKE to the soft squeak of the door.

Before I registered what was happening, Aedan sat straight up in the bed, ready for an attack.

"It's just our morning tea," I mumbled, and pulled him back down next to me under the covers.

You wouldn't have thought that a body so hard and muscled would be comfortable to sleep against.

But you'd be wrong.

"Grandfather says that he'll wait for you for breakfast," the boy blushed, "after you've finished, well, whenever you're ready."

He put the tray holding two mugs down on the dresser and rushed out of the room, dropping a bundle of fabric behind him.

Aedan laid back and laughed, long and low.

I propped my elbows on his chest and looked down at him.

For once he was smiling, completely relaxed.

How often did he get a chance to be this way?

"I think you've scared the boy," I said.

"That's not the only thing wrong with that one," he cracked. "But thankfully, it's not my problem. Come on," he said, pulling me to him for a quick kiss, then sliding out from under the covers. "I want to see how Narvin's granddaughter can manage to put a hole in my stomach lining with breakfast."

I shook my head at him.

He'd kept his pants on last night, despite my very insistent persuasion.

The evidence of his arousal pressed against me, but

as long as I was relaxed and happy, that seemed to be enough for him.

Strange man.

My brain stuttered for a moment.

Strange…something.

Along with our tea, the boy had brought loose robes up with him.

"Thoughtful," I said. "I'd meant to ask about using their laundry last night before…" I trailed off.

"Before you got distracted," Aedan smiled slyly.

"Yes. Let's just call it distracted."

Downstairs, Narvin waited for us in the kitchen.

"Give those dirty things to him," he waved to one of the kitchen helpers. "He'll brush the mud out. It's had plenty of time to dry."

"That's for certain," I said. "Thank you."

A loaf of bread twisted and filled with chopped savory spices and vegetables sat on the table, half gone.

"Wasn't about to wait for you two. Who knew when you'd be down," Narvin cackled. "Might have decided to go for another round."

My cheeks burned and it didn't matter where I looked. Knowing, amused eyes met me from everywhere.

"I want to offer you a permanent position here," Narvin announced once I'd filled my plate.

"What?" I nearly dropped the bread back on my

plate. "That's not exactly in the job description for a wandering musician."

"Then maybe you should think about a new job," the old man argued. "Other people can go from town to town getting information, spreading the news." His chin went up with pride. "Brom and Edrel are setting up an old-style printing press. Nowhere close to the tech ban, of course. Part of your job could be helping them figure out what sorts of things people want to hear about."

"But it's not the same," I said, even though part of me was fantastically curious to see the press.

"Stay in Bitters," Narvin insisted. "Flame has no authority here. Tewke's guards aren't good for much, but they can keep the peace."

I sat back in my chair. "That's what this is about? One drunk handsy guy?"

Not thinking about the attackers in the alley.

That hadn't been Kaljak's doing. Had it?

I shook my head to clear it, forcing my tone to stay light. "You know he's not the first, probably won't be the last."

"We'll see about that," Aedan said as he reached for another slice of bread.

"Besides," I added, not looking at Aedan. "I wanted to talk to you about my schedule anyway."

"Good," Narvin thumped the table. "I always knew you could see sense."

"I meant, talk to you about leaving today."

"What?" Narvin frowned. "You know you make your best money during market fair."

"I know, and I hate running out on you. But any other bard in the city would be happy to take my spot here."

It was true. Leaving early would pinch my purse. But Narvin's inn always had a good crowd. Once word got out that he didn't have a bard for the fair, other musicians would be lining up to audition.

I couldn't help glancing over at Aedan. "There's something we need to do in Lukin."

Not that I knew exactly what, but at this point, I could make a good guess.

"I was thinking," Aedan said, pushing himself back from the table. "You should stay here. I'll go take care of that errand."

I glared at him. "I thought we'd settled this."

"Well," Aedan looked uncomfortable. Awkward. Was that actually embarrassment? "Things have changed."

"Oh, they haven't changed that much, husband."

He crossed his arms over his chest. "You'd be safer if you stayed."

"Are you saying you can't protect me?"

Narvin laughed. "You may as well give up now, boy.

After three wives, I can tell you, when they've got their mind set on something, you may as well go along with it." He stood up and grabbed his crutch. "The secret to a long and happy life? Make sure your wife is happy."

"I'd be happier if she was safe," Aedan grumbled.

"Well then, you'll just have to take good care of her."

WE WENT UPSTAIRS to pack our saddlebags, while some of Narvin's grandsons went out with a shopping list for supplies and provisions, and our travel clothes were brushed out with a stiff brush.

Aedan scowled while I carefully rolled my new tunic into the saddlebag.

The scarf, it's colorful garden almost too bright, I'd keep wearing.

Slinging my retrew case over my shoulder, I grabbed my bow and headed towards the door.

Aedan didn't move. "You shouldn't come with me. You should stay here."

"Believe it or not," I said, my temper fraying, "I'm not actually your responsibility. I've taken care of myself on my own for years."

"We saw how well that worked last night," he growled. "What would you have done if I hadn't been here? Snuck out in the night again?"

That did it. "I'm going to Lukin. You can come with me, or not. Right now, I don't really care."

I reached for the door handle, but he stayed in my way, immovable. "You made your safety my responsibility," he growled.

"Well then, I can take it back," I snapped.

Dodging behind him, I went to saddle up Dayla.

"At least you're sane," I whispered to her. She ignored me, stretching behind me to reach for another mouthful of leaves.

Maybe that didn't count for much.

We didn't speak for the first hour of the trip.

I stayed on Dayla. Aedan walked beside us.

It was annoying how easily he could keep pace with her.

Except, I didn't really want to leave him behind.

What traffic there was on the road was all passing the other way, merchants and farmers heading towards Bitters, towards the market fair.

After the first hour, I shifted in the saddle and leaned down. "Aren't you coming up?"

"Didn't think you wanted me," he replied stonily.

I sighed, reached for the saddlebag that held the cut-out pieces of his new coat, and started basting them together. "No, I don't want you to assume that I'm incapable of taking care of myself."

He gave a short bark of a laugh. "I never thought it,

never said it." He didn't look up. "But if people are already after me, already know I'm on-planet, then you're safer with Narvin and his family. If I'm going to pull this off, I think..." he paused, then looked away. "I need to know you're safe."

Oh.

The admission looked like it hurt him.

"You know, I've never really worried too much about my safety," I said slowly, rotating the fabric in my hands until I found where I'd started pinning the coat.

"You shouldn't put too much faith in the custom. Just because you're a bard--"

I cut him off. "No, not because of that. Because staying safe doesn't change anything." I started sewing, focusing on the fabric, the feel of it in my hand, the steady movement of the needle. "Some things are worth the risk."

He didn't answer, and I kept sewing.

The road branched off, the larger path leading across the base of the foothills, a smaller trail running up a small valley.

"This should cut some time off, get us to Lukin about a day faster," I said, then paused, waiting for him. "Might not be as much fun for you on foot, though."

He turned towards the valley. "I wasn't really sent here to have fun." Aedan hesitated and looked back. "Is the terrain a problem for Dayla?"

Dayla followed him eagerly.

"Nope. Those back legs of hers can go up about anything. And the valley is filled with tasty things for her to eat." I turned the slowly emerging garment in my hands and started a new seam.

"There's no one listening now," I said, making a show of looking around us, but the trail was deserted. "Why don't you tell me what you're here for?"

He took a deep breath and rested one hand on Dayla's haunch to give her a scratch.

"I'm here to try to stop a war. Or worse."

AEDAN

"Somehow that seems like an odd job for you," Myria laughed, then looked shaken. "You're serious, aren't you?"

"Yeah, I'm not really the person I would've chosen for the job either," I admitted.

The trail led us through a broad valley, purple tufted trees spilling up the sides of the slopes that surrounded us.

"Flame kidnapped one of the Emperor's relatives. Flame is demanding advanced weaponry in exchange for the princess's return."

Myria shook her head slowly.

"That would completely disrupt the balance" she said, rocking along with Dayla's pace. "I'm not saying things are great now, but at least nobody's expecting the war to start all over again." Her hands fell loose in her lap, her eyes wide. "And it would, if Flame got weapons from the Emperor."

"He won't," I reassured her. "I'm here to make sure of that."

"What are you going to do by yourself?"

"Find out where he's stashed the princess, get her out, and get her home?"

"And he thinks that one man can do all that?" she asked, head cocked to the side.

If she knew everything Doc had done to us, she might not be so surprised.

Then again, thinking about how genetic engineering had been used as a weapon of terror on this planet, it was probably better that she didn't.

"It'll work out, it usually does. But I've got a little bit of a deadline."

"What happens if you miss it?" she asked, her voice small and tight.

"The Emperor comes to retrieve her himself," I answered, heart suddenly heavy at the idea. "And if you think I'm failing to blend, he won't even try."

"Right, then," she said after a long silence. "I've got a coat to finish sewing for you and you need to tell me everything." She shifted forward on the saddle. "You may as well get up here and ride. If we've got a deadline, we should pick up the pace."

A DRIZZLE of rain started midmorning. The high vaulted trees above us kept most of the water off us, but Dayla obviously disliked it.

"It's all right, girl," Myria crooned to the agitated mount. "Just think, we could be up north where it's been raining and raining for weeks."

An aggravated huff was the only answer. Apparently, that didn't fit into Dayla's likes either.

"Let's go ahead and take a break, get some lunch. I need to see how this fits on you, anyway, before I go much farther with it."

A clearing under a thick stand of trees gave us a bit more shelter, and we dismounted.

As she shook out the half-finished garment, I unhooked her bow from the saddle and began the process of taking the saddle off Dayla.

"Who's a good girl?" I said under my breath as I unbuckled the straps.

"We're not going to be here that long," Myria said.

"I know, but she's happier with it off. Aren't you, girl?" I said, rubbing under her chin. "And if we're taking a break, she should, too."

"You are *not* taking her with you when you leave," Myria teased.

A sharp pain ran through my chest.

When I left.

Left them both.

Not something I could think about.

Not now.

Not ever.

"I could," I argued, scratching the pebbled ridge above one deep onyx eye. Hell, maybe a miniature dinosaur would be an appropriate baby present. "Does Dayla have any brothers or sisters?" I asked Myria.

"Probably, but I don't even want to know what you're thinking about," she laughed. "Come here, let me try this on you and we can let Dayla eat in peace."

While Dayla wandered off in search of tasty branches, Myria wrapped the garment over my tunic and trousers.

It was long, but cut high on the sides to allow for ease of movement, with a wide sash of the same material keeping it securely closed.

I stretched my shoulders out, and the arms weren't nearly as binding as I expected them to be. "I like it," I said. "I like it a lot, actually."

"You don't need to sound so surprised."

As we finished eating, the drizzle that had followed us all morning increased, large drops of rain splashing down through the leaves.

"You may as well keep that on," Myria decided. "I

won't get much work done on it in this weather, and an extra layer won't be a bad idea."

She turned to check that the saddlebags were still tight and that the carrying case for her retrew was sealed.

"I'll need to rewax the fabric soon," she muttered. "But it should do for now." She slung it over her back, adjusting the strap on her shoulder.

A low rumble caught at the edges of my hearing. I stood, scanning the area, trying to place the noise.

"What is it?" Myria asked quietly.

I shook my head, tried to focus again on a rushing and rumbling until even Myria could hear it.

"Flash flood," she said, face paling. "We've got to make a run for it, try to get to higher ground."

"No time," I argued. "It's coming too quickly."

"But Dayla's out there!" Myria started to dash in the direction the mount had heading, but I pulled her back. "She'll have to be fine on her own. We can't worry about her now."

In the distance, near the top of the western slope, I could make out the shape of a stone hut.

We'd be safe there.

But we'd never make it.

Wrapping one arm around her waist, I leapt for the branches of the thickest tree I could see. "We've got to climb."

Grief crossed her face for a split second, then she nodded with grim understanding, realizing we had no other option.

There wasn't anywhere to hide, anywhere to run.

By now, the noise of the rushing water echoed from the sides of the valley, unmistakable, inescapable.

I pulled her with me and we climbed as high as we could.

And then the flood hit, and I knew it wasn't high enough.

"Hang on!" I shouted over the crash of water as the tree shook with the impact.

Myria clung to the trunk and I wrapped my arms around her, digging my fingers into the wood on either side to hold her safe.

The noise was deafening as the flood careened down the valley, ripping up everything in its path.

Time stretched until, with a shock of horror, I realized our haven was slowly, steadily, leaning to the side.

"Hold on, hold on," I chanted, hoping Myria could hear me over the crash and noise of the flood.

The wind whipped down the valley, knocking another tree into us. A thick branch smashed into my back and I stiffened, hoping to deflect the impact from Myria.

"I can't hold on for much longer," Myria sobbed.

"You have to," I insisted. If I had to hold her pinned to the tree until the flood was over, I would.

But then, with a sickening crack, the tree shuddered and fell, spinning down until we hit the water with a huge splash.

Another tree slammed into me, knocking me loose, tearing me away from her, dragging me under the water.

I fought my way back to the raging surface.

"Myria!" I screamed, but I couldn't see her, couldn't see anything other than rain, swirling water, and broken branches.

I dove down, searching for her, but the water was too murky, I couldn't see anything.

Clawing my way across the closest floating tree, I crouched, searching the surface of the water.

No Myria.

I sprang from one spinning log to the next, calling, searching.

Until finally, the waters receded.

The valley was a wreck, covered in mud and broken branches, with shattered trunks of trees smashed against stone.

And still, no sign of Myria.

Time stopped. Everything stopped.

I wasn't leaving until I found her.

And then I saw it, a flash of color in the muddy landscape.

The bright colors of the scarf stood out, a sad bedraggled flag.

I ran towards it, digging frantically until I found her, buried in the mud.

Amazingly, she still had her retrew with her. I tore it off her back, half wondering if the air trapped in the waxed case had saved her.

Except she wasn't breathing.

"Dammit, Myria," I shouted, turning her over to clear her airway, then pounding her back.

Nothing.

I pounded again, and she coughed, a horrid gut-wrenching sound.

The most amazing, wonderful sound I'd ever heard.

"Come on, sweetheart," I whispered to her. "Keep breathing." I stroked her back as she coughed again. "Don't leave me."

In a moment, the ragged gasps subsided, and she slumped against my chest. "We're getting out of here," I told her unconscious form.

Her face was covered in mud, bruised from where a tree branch must've hit her.

The retrew case caught my eye.

She'd want it.

Then she'd have it.

I slid it onto my own back, then lifted her, carefully cradling her in my arms as I started trudging through the mud, up the mountain, out of the destruction.

We'd lost time, and Dayla.

All our supplies.

But Myria was alive, and I had every intention of keeping her that way.

MYRIA

I woke slowly, every inch of my body feeling as if I'd been beaten.

"Easy, love," a low voice whispered to me as a cool hand stroked my hair back from my face.

It was a familiar voice, but I couldn't place it, couldn't remember where I was.

My head echoed with a rushing sound and suddenly I sat up, struggling out from under the heavy weight that covered me.

"Dayla!"

But she was gone. I knew it.

But I didn't know where I was. It was a small stone room, with tiny slit windows and a roaring fire burning merrily away in the wall opposite from where I sat.

I was undressed, but piled high with worn blankets, their combined weight pressing on me.

Confused and anxious, I pushed the blankets away and tried to get up.

"Take it easy for a minute, would you?"

I blinked and looked away from the light, then I saw Aedan sitting on a stool by the head of the bed.

"You look like hell," I said with an involuntary gasp.

I was naked under the blankets, but he was still in his trousers, the new brown coat and his original shirt both drying by the fire next to my clothing.

Mud had caked in his hair, but what worried me was his eyes.

When we'd met, he'd been cold, aloof. I'd seen him amused, angry.

Lethal.

But I'd never seen him worried and worn.

"What's wrong?" I said, reaching a hand towards him.

He sank to his knees beside the bed and dragged me into his lap. "I thought you were dead. I couldn't protect you, and you trusted me to."

I pushed away and cupped my hand over his cheek. "You can't protect me from everything. That's what I've been trying to tell you."

His jaw set stubbornly. "I should be able to. If I'd tried harder, if I--"

"What are you going to do, make the rain fall somewhere else? Keep trees from falling, floods from happening?"

I didn't seem to be getting through to him. Or he thought all those things should be possible, if he'd just worked harder.

"I'm sorry about Dayla," he said, wrapping his arms around me, bringing me against the warmth of his chest. "She was a good friend."

I sniffled, just a little.

"Torwynn are smart. We don't know what happened to her for sure." I imagined her running, scared and alone. "Maybe she escaped, maybe she found another herd, will go off to have her own adventures."

Aedan nuzzled the top of my head.

"As long as she doesn't try to eat somebody else's hair. Still, I'm sorry."

I pushed away and wiped my tears.

"You can't keep me safe from everything. I don't know what it's like out there where you're from." I pulled back, fighting with the water-swollen tie that had knotted in my hair. "Is it all perfect, all peaceful up there in the stars?"

"No," he grunted. "Anything but."

"Then why do you think it'd be different down here?"

He didn't answer, just stroked my hair.

"We don't have forever." I whispered the words into his chest. "We don't even have a season, do we?"

He stretched out in front of the fire and pulled me down to lie across him.

"No," he admitted reluctantly. "I have six days now."

"And then what?" I asked, my voice small.

"It'll be alright, I promise."

I shook my head angrily. "You can't make promises like that."

In a flash he rolled, bringing me with the movement so that I was pinned beneath him.

His eyes were the wild blue I'd seen in the market.

Feral.

Hungry.

"I can and will promise you this. I will keep you safe."

"And once you leave?" I whispered.

"Maybe I don't have to leave," he said, his lips so close to my face that they brushed my skin with every word.

"I wouldn't want to make you stay," I gasped, burning at his touch.

"You could make me do anything," he murmured, breath hot against the shell of my ear.

I groaned as he kissed my neck.

"I thought I'd lost you."

"I'm right here." I strained against his hold, eager to touch him, to run my hands down his chest.

Wriggling, I freed one hand and trailed my fingers down his muscled side.

He squirmed.

"You're ticklish!" I announced gleefully.

"Oh no, you don't," he growled, but I danced my fingers down his side until he squirmed again.

He gave me just enough room to slide my hand down the front of his trousers, to feel his hard length.

"Myria," he moaned, "stop that."

"No," I said simply.

I nudged him to his back, and he lay rigid, panting as I stroked him harder through the fabric.

His eyes closed, and only the faintest tremor showed how close his control was to snapping.

"Why do you think I would possibly want to stop," I murmured, dropping kisses up his stomach, across his broad chest, until I could nuzzle in the hollow of his neck.

"You don't know what I am," his words no more than breath in the air.

"I know enough," I countered.

I slid my fingers inside the waistband of his pants, just enough to brush the broad head of his cock.

"I know that I want to do this. And unless I'm terribly mistaken, you want me, too."

At the next touch, he reared up and dragged me onto his lap, my bent legs on either side of his waist.

No gentle kisses now, but taking, plundering my mouth, twining my tongue with his own as his hands ran up and down the bare, fire-warmed skin of my back.

Suddenly, the fingers of one hand gripped the curve of my ass and he ground me against his rigid cock.

I shivered against his chest, and he did it again, thrusting against my throbbing clit until the wave crashed over me, his kisses swallowing my screams.

Before I realized it, his pants were off and he lay over me, the firelight flickering across his skin like a god, like a demon.

Like something this world had never seen.

I reached for him and he fell upon me, his hands and mouth everywhere, up and down my body, my breasts, my thighs until the breath caught in my throat, the spiral of desire hotter than flame.

Desperate, panting, I cried out as he finally penetrated me, driving into me with unbridled need.

"Mine," he growled. "And nothing, no one will take you from me. Say it," he insisted, his words pummeling me with every thrust.

"Yes," I panted, the wave of sensations spiraling through me, forcing the words from my lips that I never would've admitted. "Yours."

And I was.

And he was mine, just as surely.

For now.

THE MORNING CAME, clear and bright.

I did my best to brush the mud off our traveling clothes.

"At least your new coat survived." I checked the stitching, pleased that it had held up so well. "But my pretty new tunic," I fussed. Given everything we had lost, it was silly to be upset about it.

But I was.

"I'll buy you another," he nuzzled my neck. "As soon as all of this is over."

But my stomach remained in a cold knot.

When all of this was over.

Well, we'd see.

I still had my lovely scarf, a little faded from the mud, but the colors were still lovely to my eye.

"If we go straight across the mountains, we should be able to make up the time." Braiding my hair quickly, I pulled on my boots and slung my retrew case over my shoulder. "I've got some friends in Lukin, maybe they can help find your princess."

Aedan snorted. “She’s not my princess, but I’ll take whatever help I can get.”

I threw open the door and there, waiting for us, was an unexpected sight.

“Dayla!” I cried out, throwing my arms around her neck, not even caring if she scratched me with those talons.

“Who’s a smart girl? Such a clever girl,” Aedan cooed at her.

Seriously.

Cooed.

“You were just as worried about her as I was,” I accused him.

“Maybe.”

And he didn’t look ashamed of it at all.

“While I’m happy to see you, girl,” I said, “I can’t ride without a saddle.” I looked at the short, curved spines that ran down her back. “We’ll get you a new one in Lukin, but for now you can just keep us company.”

“Let me see what I can do,” Aedan said, disappearing back into the hut. In moments, he emerged with half the blankets.

“You can’t take those,” I insisted. “This is some poor shepherd’s hut. Just because he’s moved a flock of tessa into town for the market fair doesn’t mean he won’t be back, won’t want his blankets.”

Aedan shrugged. “I suspect I left far more coin than

the blankets are worth. But check, I'm never sure with local currency."

I went back into the hut. He was right. The shepherd probably wouldn't be upset, not in the slightest.

With that in mind, I rummaged through the small cupboard.

"Well, they won't be tasty." I held out a small stack of travel biscuits that had been wrapped in cloth.

Probably forgotten in the hustle and bustle of getting the flock ready for market.

"But considering everything else got lost in the flood, we'll take them."

Aedan took one, gnawed off a corner. "What in the Void are these made from?" His nose wrinkled. "Never mind, I don't want to know."

"Good decision."

I thought about where we were, trying to remember what trails were in the area.

"If we keep heading north and east, we should be in Lukin by the end of the day. We'll get something a little more edible there."

"If we can't," Aedan said, tearing one blanket into strips and braiding it into a rope to fasten the pad he'd made from the others onto Dayla's back, "I don't think much of your friends."

What would he think of my friends anyway? I wondered.

We'd soon find out.

The makeshift saddle slid a bit, but Dayla seemed to understand that we didn't have much choice but to make do.

Her huge, three-toed feet strolled easily across the muddy expanse. Aedan jogged forward and then back, scouting safe paths, always keeping us in sight.

I would never have been able to keep up with either of them.

As we covered the landscape, I checked on the retrew.

Two strings had snapped, but the wood hadn't cracked. I ran my fingers down the sides, checking the curve of the instrument for warping.

It felt fine, but I wouldn't really be able to tell until I tried to play it.

"Going to get some practice in?" Aedan asked as he came back to my side once more.

"I don't think your coin will last forever," I said. "I better get some of my own, just as soon as I can get this restrung."

As we were about to crest the next rise, Aedan stiffened.

"What is it?" I asked, unable to keep the tremor from my voice. Not another flood. Please no.

"Nothing bad. I don't think so, at least," he said hastily. "Is there another town here? Or a tavern?"

I thought, tried to place us on the map I carried in my head. "Maybe a couple of homesteads, but no, nothing like a village."

"Maybe we'll see if they can get us something to eat better than those travel biscuits you found."

"Who would've thought you were such a picky eater," I teased him.

But all thoughts of food fled from both of us as we crested the rise.

The flood hadn't hit this valley.

But the once-neat farm below us still hadn't been spared.

"What happened here?" I wondered. "Lightning?

Aedan shook his head. "No, this was nothing natural." He hurried down to the burned-out farmhouse and I followed.

"An accident, I hope. Sometimes the chimneys on old stoves get blocked. It happened at least once that I can remember in my old village." I was chattering, rambling.

Whatever had happened here, there was still an unpleasant aura over the site.

I didn't like it.

"I doubt it. I can smell men, lots of them." He glanced at me, then away. "Someone familiar."

"Who would do something like this? And what do

you mean, familiar?" I started to question him, then heard a soft cry.

Aedan sprinted towards where a wall had half collapsed, forming a lean-to of stone and rubble.

"Stand back," he ordered, and for once I didn't think to argue.

I stepped to the side as he began testing rocks, pulling them off one by one quickly, but not so fast that the whole mess came tumbling down.

"Keep talking," he called out to whoever was underneath. "We're almost there."

I saw a small hand first.

Then a shock of brown hair atop a small, heart-shaped face, with tear tracks cutting through the glaze of ash and dust.

With infinite care, Aedan pulled her out and handed her to me.

A little girl, no more than six.

Wide brown eyes looked back and forth between us.

"Do you know where my momma is?"

"No, sweetie," I knelt down in the ash next to her. "I don't know her, I don't think. What's your mom's name?"

She frowned, obviously disturbed by my nonsense. "Momma."

Of course.

"What's your name?"

She sniffled, swallowed back tears. “Sweetie.”

“Oh, you’re such a good girl, Sweetie, being so brave.” One more try for information, something, anything. “What happened here?”

“I think the bad men took her,” she whispered. “She told me to hide. And then there was screaming. And the fire.”

Aedan’s face was grim. “We need to keep moving. Get her up on Dayla with you.”

“But surely someone must’ve seen something, there must be more family, friends, neighbors,” I argued, not able to wrap my mind around this.

“No time,” he said. “I’d rather take her back to Narvin, but for now, we’ll have to bring her along with us.” Without waiting, he tightened the fabric straps around Dayla, then lifted me up to her back and handed me the child.

Quickly, he rummaged through the ruins of the house, somehow finding enough food to last the three of us for a day. But nothing more.

“Now we run.”

AEDAN

It wasn't just the burned farmhouse.

It wasn't just the stench of a troop of men laid over the ash, or the scent of the terrified woman that had been dragged away, but also the tickle in the back of my skull that urged me to get away from there as quickly as possible. .

There was something else going on here besides the kidnapped princess. Something else I didn't know about.

And while I might not have Connor's telepathy or Xander's predictions, I could play a hunch well enough.

If I didn't move, my timeline was about to get shorter.

Dayla kept up with me just fine as Myria held the

child close to her, speaking softly to the tiny head above the small hands that clung to her traveling coat.

"Aedan," Myria called to me after two hours had passed. "We need to stop."

As if she understood the words of her rider, Dayla slowed and came to a stop under a broadly spreading tree.

"Here, take her for a moment."

I reached up to take the still silent child while Myria stiffly climbed down.

"I'm sorry," Myria said, stretching her back. "You did a fantastic job rigging the blankets up like that." She shook out one leg, then the other, grimacing a bit. "But my backside really misses my old saddle."

I took a moment to appreciate said body part.

"Well, I wouldn't want anything to—"

I glanced down at the child.

Shut my mouth.

"Do you need to stretch, too?"

Silence.

Right, then. Small children weren't really my thing. I tried to hand the little girl back to Myria, but her tiny fists clenched my jacket, refusing to let go.

"Hey, kiddo, wouldn't you like to go back to the nice lady? Her name is Myria, and she's a really good singer."

No answer.

"Did you see her pretty scarf?"

Nothing.

"Do you want to see her instrument? I bet she'd let you play with it."

Still no answer, but this time I got a glare from Myria.

Void. Maybe I should have spent more time with Vicki, tried to figure out some tips for the toddler set.

I glanced down again, to find wide eyes studying me curiously.

Myria leaned over. "Is there anybody we should ask for when we get to Lukin?" She brushed the hair out of the child's eyes. "Your father, your grandparents, maybe?"

Sweetie shook her head still refusing to speak. Fine. I shifted her to one side and used my free arm to check on Dayla's straps.

"They'll hold for a few more hours," I decided. "How much longer until—Ow!"

A sharp tug at my scalp stopped my thought in its tracks.

I glared at Dayla, but she continued innocently grazing at the bright purple bushes.

While I was distracted, the child had wormed her way up to my shoulders and grabbed handfuls of my hair.

"Hey, kiddo, you gotta get down," I said. Calmly. I'm sure it was calmly.

"Pretty!" she said.

Great. Just great.

"I kinda like it, too," Myria told her. "Your hair has approval with three out of three ladies in our party."

I reached both arms over my head to try to get a grip on Sweetie, but she ducked back down, crouching on my back.

"Myria," I called. Calmly. "Could you do something about this?"

She leaned against a tree, hands over her face. "I am. I'm laughing." She wiped her eyes. "It feels really good, you know?"

"At the moment, no. No, I don't." I reached back again, and missed the child once more. "Come on down, Sweetie. I'll go find you something else pretty, okay? Something not attached to my scalp?"

I looked around wildly.

Surely there was something else that would distract a little girl.

Something soft and fluffy. I glanced at Dayla's pebbly hide.

Maybe not fluffy.

Something bright and … there!

A thick vine curled around a tree, covered with large yellow and teal striped blooms.

"Let's get you some of these, instead," I said, reaching forward just as Myria shouted a warning.

I was still pulling out thin, needle-like spines from my hand when we continued on the trail.

But Sweetie had her carefully dethorned flower, and was apparently quite pleased with it.

She sat with Myria, perched high on Dayla's back, but throughout the last hours of the ride, her hand leaned towards me, as if to show me the bloom all over again.

"Pretty," she announced.

"Yes, I said it is pretty. I'm glad you like it."

By evening, we'd started to leave the treeline behind, the landscape becoming rockier, craggy, the ground covered in loose shale that Dayla kicked up in annoyance.

As we came to the last stand of trees, we looked over a short valley. Myria stopped and pointed.

"There it is."

Lukin.

Halfway up the next rise, a high wall circled the town, three or four times the size of Bitters. It looked as if it had been planted on the top of a chopped-off mountain, with a tall wall surrounding it, just to give it that extra cozy feel.

A single trail led to a guarded gate.

And in the middle, on a slight rise, stood a towering castle, looming over the entire town. It was a huge stone cube, with a blocky tower on each corner.

"Don't know how I feel about wandering up and announcing ourselves," I said. "Will our travel papers from Bitters work here? Can we add Sweetie, or will they not notice the kid?"

Myria shook her head. "Flame doesn't have the same restrictions on travel that some of the other towns do. But he searches and questions travelers. We're going to have to come up with a good story."

I looked at her and the child on Dayla. "Can we just say we're a family on holiday? Off to see the sights?"

Myria laughed. "We could try that. And then you could rescue us, too."

"Charming. Well, let's get closer and think about it. Something will come up."

But as we got closer, the something that came up was another problem.

Each visitor to the town was stopped and questioned thoroughly.

And then the guards brought out a box. Nothing scary or intimidating, just a metal box.

The travelers put their hand in the box and even from down the trail, I could hear the high-pitched whine it made.

Dayla shook her head violently, forcing Myria to clutch the makeshift saddle for balance.

"It's not Dayla's fault, but you may want to get

down," I said quickly. "I don't think she likes that noise any more than I do."

"What noise?" Myria asked as she dismounted, but I noticed that Sweetie's face was scrunched up, her flower crumpled tightly in her hand.

"That box. I don't know where Flame got it from, but I'm willing to bet that's some sort of biometric scanner."

"A bio what?" Myria asked, holding tightly to Sweetie. "Is it some kind of weapon?"

I shook my head. "It's a bit of tech, not that advanced really, but more than anything else I've seen here. And in its most basic form, it can identify every individual person who comes in and out of that gate."

"That doesn't sound too bad," Myria said, but I continued on, making the plan.

"You and Sweetie take Dayla and get through the gates. I'll meet you somewhere inside." That should work. "You've played in taverns in Lukin before, just tell me the spot, and I'll be there." I remembered the odd sign in front of Narvin's. "You might have to describe the critter, though."

"That's nonsense," Myria argued. "What are you going to do, climb the wall?"

"Not until after dark," I said. "It's not really that tall."

She threw a hand into the air. "So they'll know we

came in through the gate. Lots of travelers do. There's nothing to mark us as anything out of the ordinary."

I didn't answer, but she knew there was something wrong.

She narrowed her eyes. "What, do they have different kinds of fingerprints in the Empire?"

I looked away. "Something like that."

Myria was silent for a long minute.

"Well, if you can't get through the gate, we need to come up with an alternate route. We're not splitting up, not now."

She put Sweetie down, then turned her back on the city and began unfastening the straps from Dayla's back.

"What are you doing?" I asked.

"I think there's another way in. But Dayla can't go with us."

"No," I argued. "I'm not going to make you leave her out here. We don't even know what's out in these mountains."

Myria stopped to stroke Dayla's head, but quickly kept moving, untying the last of the braided fabric ropes. "She's smart. She's fast. She survived the flood in better shape than we did." Another pat down Dayla's muzzle. "She'll be fine."

I grabbed Sweetie from where she'd started

climbing up a teetering pile of rocks, obviously looking for something else pretty and pokey.

"Where do you think we're going, that we can't take Dayla but Sweetie will be safe?" I asked.

Myria turned around, clumsily coiling the rope up, her shoulders still leaning against Dayla's hide.

"It's not a matter of being safe. It's a matter of fitting. There are tunnels. From somewhere on the side of the mountain, straight into the city."

I blinked. "That's stupid."

"What do you mean?"

"Think about it." I pointed across the valley. "Someone has gone to the trouble of putting the city on the top of a mountain, with a giant wall all the way around it, with one gate, with guards…and there's tunnels that go right underneath?"

Myria cocked an eyebrow. "I didn't say they were unguarded."

MYRIA

"*When the moon shines brightly, on the windswept valley.*

And the tangled thras vines, wrap the hills."

"This is it," I decided. "The settlement has got to be around here."

We had circled back the way we'd come, searching for another path around the mountain that Lukin crouched on.

"The creek, the boulder that looks like a woman." I pointed, looking for more landmarks.

Aedan studied the rock formation doubtfully.

"It looks like a boulder."

"Trust me, this has to be the location."

Bards have a network of information.

Not everything gets passed on when we're sharing news.

Sometimes it's private, only of interest to one or two people.

Sometimes it's so sensational that it can't be believed.

And sometimes it's a rumor, the ghost of a story.

The barest bones of a story that needed to be fleshed out.

Maybe you'd get one bit of information in one town, hear a little bit more three months later somewhere else.

And never be entirely sure.

The tunnels under Lukin were something like that.

An older woman I met in my first year of apprenticeship had given me the clue.

She'd come from Lukin.

Well, almost.

"The warlord tore down all the houses, razed them to the ground so there was no trace, my grandmother said." It had been years ago, but I remembered her clearly. Shorter than I was, broad, solidly built, face tough.

"My family had been running that damn mine since the colony was settled." She'd turned and kicked at the fire, in a tavern in my memory. "Didn't make a damn bit of difference in the end."

Before the war, there'd been a settlement for the workers that used the fancy excavator machines winding their way deep into the mountain, pulling out ore that seemed to go back into the manufacturing of more of those machines, and more tech.

And weapons.

And I guess things like that scanner that had Aedan so spooked.

The warlords had used the drillers as weapons, plowing them through enemy lines until their energy cells wore out.

Flame had built his citadel at the top of the mountain, taking advantage of the leveled stone, and a city sprang up around it.

But the tunnels were still there, underneath.

"I'll admit, there could've been a settlement here," Aedan looked around at the shelf of land cut into the mountainside.

"But how did they get into the tunnels?"

As the darkness fell, we searched, until finally Sweetie's endless curiosity about flowers found it.

It was under the thras vines. Should have paid more attention to the song.

An oval opening was cut into the rock, large enough for Aedan to easily pass through.

Or, it would have been, except for the heavy metal grate that blocked the passage.

My heart sank.

"We can find another way. There's always another way, right?"

"Sure there is." Aedan stepped forward, grabbed the bars, and pulled.

With a screech of metal that resounded through the hillside, he yanked it free and tossed it to the side.

"There's our other way."

NUDGE.

"Stop it," I whispered for the twentieth time to Dayla.

If anyone thought that torwynn were tamed creatures that allowed you to ride them wherever you wanted to go and didn't have any thoughts or opinions of their own on the matter, obviously they had never spent time with one.

Nudge.

"I swear…" I muttered and Sweetie popped her head up over Aedan's shoulder from where he was carrying her down into the tunnels.

"Don't swear. Naughty." She ducked back down, leaving me to glare at Dayla in silence the next time the torwynn nudged my shoulder with her massive head, knocking the retrew case sideways on my back every time.

This had not been the plan.

The plan had been to free Dayla to rejoin her herd, to have other adventures somewhere safer.

The plan had been that I'd carry Sweetie while Aedan roamed ahead, since apparently the faintly luminescent grubs that covered the walls were enough for him to see clearly.

I stumbled along, barely able to make out his dark shape ahead of me.

Dayla had shoved her way behind us, folding those long legs further than I'd ever seen a torwynn manage before, filling the tunnel completely.

And Sweetie had decided that she was going to ride on Aedan.

I'd seen enough children in my travels.

Unless we wanted to risk high-pitched screams of anger echoing underneath the city, we'd have to let her stay with him.

"For now. If something happens, you have to go back to Myria and Dayla," Aedan had explained patiently.

She nodded solemnly.

Apparently, that flower had been worth a lot of kiddy trust.

Slowly, we worked our way deeper into the mountain.

“You said this was guarded,” Aedan’s whisper echoed in the dark. “What exactly should I be expecting?”

“I have no idea, but it makes sense there’d be something down here.” I shrugged, even if he couldn’t see me. “It’s not like Flame could just collapse the mines, the city would fall.” I ran my hand down the smooth wall.

Whatever they’d used to tunnel through the solid rock was amazing. No sharp tool marks, just smoothly undulating stone.

Aedan paused. The passageway we traveled continued straight ahead, but another veered off to the right.

“Which way do you think we should take?” I wondered.

“This looks like the main shaft,” he said, rubbing his hand over the corner of stone.

“Look at the cutting pattern,” he pointed to a ripple in the stone. “This passage was made first, and then the other was cut through it.”

I peered into the gloom, but couldn’t see. Dayla shoved her head over my shoulder to stare into the darkness, but apparently, she didn’t like it either.

“I’ll take your word for it.” I kept moving and caught

up to his long strides. "Either way, this one leads up. It'll have to come out somewhere."

Only our muffled footsteps broke the heavy silence, until finally the dark and quiet got to me.

"What is it really like, out there in the stars?" I'd dreamed about it as a kid. Flying away to different worlds, all the amazing things that must be possible.

I'd tried to stop dreaming about it, but there was always that little speck of wonder and excitement.

Aedan's shoulders stiffened.

"It's a mess," he said finally. "The Empire lost its way and a lot of people paid the price." He sighed. "The new guy will probably be pretty good, if politics doesn't corrupt him."

"Not that it'll make any difference to us," I said.

"It might," Aedan argued. "I don't like the guy particularly, but I think he means well. And he thinks he knows your planet was treated badly before. If he gets a chance to try to fix things, he will."

I turned over his words in my head.

"That sounded like you know the Emperor. I can't imagine that's normal for everyday soldiers, is it?"

He snorted. "I'm not exactly in anyone's army. Or normal. And, yeah, somehow he's best friends with my brother's mate."

Somehow, all of his answers just made more questions. "Is she a princess, too?"

"Nope, just beats his—" a quick glance at Sweetie caught his attention, "backside at video games and calls him on his nonsense. Someone has to do it."

And even more questions.

But all of them washed out of my mind as the tunnel made a gentle curve, and up ahead...

"What's that light?" I whispered. "We can't be above ground this quickly, could we? And it would still be night, I'm sure of it."

Without a word, Aedan handed me Sweetie and motioned for us to stay still.

I fell back, pressed against Dayla's side, and waited, but within moments, he returned.

"You're going to love this."

The tunnel opened up into a large cavern, tunnels radiating off it like spokes in a wheel, the ceiling soaring above us. Arches of stone curved from the floor of the chamber, spiraling up to new openings high up in the side of the wall.

Only one bridge had broken, chunks of stone littering the floor where the stone span had snapped.

Small glowing globes of soft yellow dotted the surfaces, their light steadily burning as it must have for decades.

"This's amazing," I gasped. "This must run through half the mountain." And then it clicked. "How are the lights still shining?"

Aedan walked to the closest one and sniffed at it. "Irocian power source. It'll run nearly forever."

It was hard to tell what was stranger, light that could burn forever, or that he could tell how it was powered by scent.

Even more questions, that would probably never be answered, so I turned to the more practical. "I wonder what else is down here. Maybe there's tools that were left, something we could use."

Sweetie kicked to be let down, and immediately ran to Dayla's side to trace the stripes across her haunches.

"Her claws are sharp! Don't let her hug you."

There were sentences I had never expected to say. That was one of them.

"Pretty Dayla," Sweetie answered, and kept stroking the torwynn, who didn't seem to mind in the slightest.

Well, at least some things didn't change, even if there was a possible stash of hidden tech right in front of us.

While Aedan investigated the tunnels and checked for signs only he could see, I roamed the cavern.

Maybe the lights weren't the only thing that had been left behind. Even if there was nothing else, if I could get one of those lights off the wall, that would be handy.

"What would you do if you did find something?" Aedan asked from right behind me.

How could someone so large move so quietly? It just wasn't right.

"I don't know," I admitted. "But it seems like such a waste. Unlimited power keeping the lights on in a cave, when every day, just heating water is a struggle."

"Fair enough," he said. "I just wonder what this world is going to do when high technology is reintroduced."

I whirled toward him. "What do you mean? They arrest people for the ban all the time."

"That doesn't ever seem to stop progress," he said as he moved towards another of the branching corridors. "Narvin's sons are setting up a printing press. Somebody figured out how to do a bioscanner. No one erases progress, not completely." He tilted his head, listening. "The trick is going to be to make sure that it's not only people like Flame that keep all the toys."

"About that," I started. "I've been meaning to tell you--"

I fell silent at the quick motion of his hand.

He loped across the room and handed me his knife. "Get the child."

I grabbed Sweetie, and wished again for my bow. It was probably washed to the sea already, carried away by the flood.

"I know what you can do without a weapon, but

we've really got to get me a knife when we get into town."

"Yeah, I know. I'll put it on the list of things we ought to do."

There wasn't a good way to carry a child and wield a knife. At least, not for me.

"Let's try this."

Sweetie's small form fit snugly between the top ridges of Dayla's spines, and she clutched with tiny fingers at the crude harness I fashioned from the braided fabric.

I held Dayla's muzzle between my hands and stared into her eyes. "I think you understand me, at least a little. I've always suspected you did." This was probably ridiculous, but just in case, it was worth it. "If you've ever paid attention, please move slowly, don't let her slide off."

Of course, there was no answer.

Just another "pretty!" from Sweetie.

I sighed. We were going to have to work on a bigger vocabulary, as soon as we weren't in these tunnels. "Yes, honey, Dayla is very pretty."

"No," the child insisted, pointing over my head to the tunnel behind me. "Pretty."

I turned, bracing for whatever horror had caught Aedan's attention, set him on the alert.

But this time, Sweetie was right.

"It's just a flock of tessa." I breathed a sigh of relief. "How did they get down here?"

Aedan backed away slowly as a dozen knee-high pink-and-purple-spotted, soft, rounded shapes approached him rapidly. "Are you sure these are what you pointed out to me outside of Bitters?"

"Yeah, tessa. They eat all kinds of plants, even weeds, and are pretty gentle. Friend of mine back home had one for a pet when I was a kid."

He shot me a quick glance and kept backing towards us. "We need to talk about your childhood."

"Why?" I blinked, bewildered. "Tessa are sweet. Maybe we should get one for Sweetie."

And then they attacked.

High-pitched keening filled the cavern as their lips drew back, baring sharp, jagged teeth.

"What the hell is that!" I exclaimed, stumbling away.

"That's not what they're supposed to look like up close?" Aedan asked as he snatched one out of the air that was leaping towards us and flung it away.

"No!" I shouted. "Tessa are cute. Snuggly!"

"Yeah, that's what you said," he shouted back. "But I've learned not to assume what women's idea of cute is," he added as he kicked another away.

"I don't know if I want to meet the other women in your life," I said as I slashed down towards one that had come far too close to my boots.

Hampered by the need to be careful with Sweetie on her back, Dayla's movements were slow, but she was still able to lean forward just enough that her talons caught another attacking not-tessa, slicing across its throat.

"I don't know," Aedan called back. "I think you'd actually get along with them."

Individually, the creatures, whatever they were, weren't a threat.

But as more and more of them flooded the chamber, I began to worry.

We fought them off, Aedan kicking and throwing them against the hard wall, where they lay stunned until they shook themselves, then rose again.

I slashed and stabbed the ones that came too close to Dayla and Sweetie.

And then Dayla entered the fight.

"No, where are you going? That's not what we talked about!" I yelled.

Aedan froze for a moment to look at me. "You didn't really make battle plans with her, did you?"

"Of course not, I just talk to her sometimes," I shouted while chasing a not-tessa away from Dayla.

"Tell me when she starts answering."

A sharp pain stabbed through my calf, and I swung low to stab at the one who'd bitten me.

It fell away, squealing, but two more swarmed, taking its place.

This wasn't going to end well.

Aedan's skills didn't matter. My bow wouldn't have made a difference, or more knives.

Not against numbers like this.

There had to be another way.

AEDAN

"Aedan!"

At Myria's shout, ice-cold panic ran through me.

Battling through the crowd of little pink monsters, I'd found myself with one of the shattered stone blocks between us.

I raced towards her, kicking the biting, clawing things out of the way.

But they were fine.

If I didn't know better, I would say that Dayla was actually watching Myria's back.

Maybe not doing the best job, but she swiped and snapped at anything within reach, keeping one beady black eye on the movement behind them, while Myria did her best to keep the ground clear in the front.

Her pants leg had been torn, an ugly gash bleeding freely. The brightly colored scarf around her neck only made her face look grayer.

She waved off my concern. "I have a plan, but I need to know what you can do." She looked steadily at me. "What you can really do."

"Well, um, you know, I'm a reasonably good fighter and… this wasn't really the moment I'd expected to get into this."

"No," she argued. "I'm not stupid, and I'm not going to freak out, but I need the truth."

Myria pointed to the gap in the broken arch above us. "Can you jump that length?"

"Yes," I answered flatly.

And once I did, it would be over between us.

No fully human man could make that jump.

And Myria had made it clear how she felt about genetic modifications when we'd fought the creature in the river.

"Good." She nodded. "Can you jump it while carrying me?"

"Of course. I wouldn't go anywhere without you." I smiled and tried to keep my voice light, but I knew that my answer meant it was over between us.

"Perfect."

I thought for a moment, estimating tonnage. "I don't think I could take Dayla, though, but I could try."

Finally, Myria looked shocked. "I wasn't going to ask you to. Dayla can take care of herself. I just need to get her pointed in the right direction."

Myria took the makeshift reins from Sweetie's hands and pulled them over the torwynn's head. "Just hold tight right here," she instructed as she wrapped the tiny fingers around one of the spines.

Sweetie had stopped calling the pink monsters pretty, but she didn't seem to be overly worried about the entire situation. I didn't know if that was a good or a bad thing.

"Come on, Dayla, this way," Myria said. "Aedan, can you do something about these?" she waved her free hand at the crowd of not-tessa between her and the base of the bridge.

Happily.

I might not understand exactly what the plan was, but I could keep those things away from Myria and Dayla as they picked their way across the cavern.

"Up you go, girl." Myria walked backward onto the bridge, still leading Dayla, who seemed to look at the whole thing as an interesting trick she was being asked to perform.

A sudden thought struck me. "Are you sure the arch will bear her weight?"

Myria's face paled. "I hadn't thought of that. It'll

have to hold her. I don't think there's another way out of this."

I hated to admit it, but I agreed with her.

Our options were limited, and dwindling.

Quickly, Myria took the remaining braided rope and fastened Sweetie as securely as possible to Dayla's back.

"Come on, we've got to go."

Slowly, the four of us made our way up the bridge.

"We need to stop here," I said as we approached the gap. "Even I need a little bit of a running start."

Myria checked Sweetie's harness. "You stay here with Dayla. In a minute, Aedan will be back to get you, alright?"

Myria turned back to me. "And once Sweetie is over, I can call for Dayla, and we'll all be on the other side. Easy."

But her eyes were wide, as if she was still convincing herself this was a good idea.

"Sure," I said, "but what happens when we get there?"

"For a start, we won't be swarmed by the not-tessas."

"That's a good point," I conceded. "Fine, let's go."

She gave a little gasp as I lifted her into my arms.

The not-tessas swarmed at the base of the bridge as if not entirely sure how to start the ascent.

I took a moment to breathe deeply of her hair, taking in the scent of her.

If I was right, this would be the last time I would touch her like this, hold her in my arms.

"Hold tight," I said.

And we were off.

My feet pounded on the stone surface, and suddenly, we were in midair.

Myria's shriek barely had time to leave her lips before we were safely on the other side.

I set her down gently, then turned to make the return trip for Sweetie.

"No!" Myria screamed.

For Dayla, faithful torwynn that she was, had decided not to wait.

She charged up the arch of the bridge, aiming straight towards us, either undeterred or spurred on by Sweetie's howls of delight.

And then she jumped.

"Oh no oh no oh no oh no," Myria chanted.

"BACK UP!" I shouted, grabbing her, pulling her with me as we retreated deeper into the tunnel.

Because Myria had been right. There was no need to worry about Dayla's jumping ability.

And given the delighted grin on Sweetie's face, we'd have trouble convincing the two of them not to do it again.

"I REALLY WISH we could've taken one of those lanterns," Myria said.

It had been hours of following the tunnel up through the dark. The glow worms apparently hadn't colonized this level.

I could tell we were still in the same tunnel, though faint breezes indicated side passages, but even my vision had trouble picking out much detail. For now, we'd stay in the main tunnel, with its steady incline, but I made a mental note of where the branches were, in case they were useful.

"Is the kid still asleep?" I whispered.

Using the sturdy coat Myria had sewn for me, we'd fashioned a smaller pad, with enough fabric left over to wrap the child up securely. Sweetie had nestled against Dayla's neck and fallen asleep.

The quiet was a relief for both of us, but we knew it wouldn't last.

"What are we going to do with her?" Myria asked.

"I don't know," I answered. "But that homestead didn't look like it saw a lot of visitors. We couldn't leave her there."

"I know, I just worry."

As we ascended, the passageway curved and slowly became perceptibly lighter. "There's something ahead."

"Do you think it's another cavern like the last one?" Myria asked. "Maybe we can take a light or two from there."

"As long as it's not filled with knee-high, pink carnivorous puffballs, I'll be happy."

"There you go, always wanting things," she teased, and for a moment the knot in my chest, the worry about what might have changed between us, eased.

Then it clicked. We weren't approaching a lighted cavern. The lights were moving towards us.

"Get back!" I whispered urgently. "Back to the last side tunnel!"

Then we realized that the same long legs that allowed Dayla to leap such distances were simply not built for trying to go backwards.

With agonizing slowness, we maneuvered Dayla and the still-sleeping Sweetie back into the last side tunnel. Myria crouched tensely just through the opening, waiting.

I crept back up the tunnel, towards the glow of the lights, still close enough that I could hear Myria's breathing.

Far enough away that a battle shouldn't wake Sweetie. Not if I was fast.

And I was usually very fast.

The sounds of men's footfalls echoed from the stone walls. Whoever they were, they'd be useful.

They'd have light we could take, and hopefully, more weapons.

And I'd be able to track their scents back to the city, get us up out of these damn tunnels.

Back pressed against the wall, I waited until they were within reach, and then I sprang.

Three of them, the back of my mind processed while I grabbed for the first, hurled him away. Two younger, holding torches. Front and back.

Middle position, an older man, gray hair and beard, looking down at a box.

Not a box. Some sort of scanner, or a sensor. Either way, tech that shouldn't be here.

Void.

The one I'd thrown hit the far side of the tunnel, his torch spinning out of his hands.

The second, younger man pushed in front of the gray beard, brandishing his torch at me like a weapon.

"Stay back!" he shouted.

Idiot. If that racket had woken up Sweetie, Myria was going to be pissed.

I threw him further than the first one.

One more to incapacitate, then I'd be able to finish them off quietly.

I grabbed the older one by the throat, ready to bash his head against the wall.

"Aedan, stop!" Myria shouted.

What?

"Stop, please," she cried, and rested her hand on my arm. "I know these guys."

"Why the hell would you know people wandering around in the dark in a tunnel?" I snapped.

She shot me a look.

Oh.

"These are my friends, the ones in Lukin that I wanted you to meet." She squeezed a little harder on my arm. "The ones I think might have information for you?"

Well, this was awkward.

I released my grip and the man sank to his knees, gasping for air.

Myria hurried to his side, wrapping her arm around his shoulders. "Grohl, are you all right?"

"Who is this, what are you doing here?" he sputtered.

"We were trying to get into the city, but going in the front door seemed like a bad idea."

"You could have been killed down here," he wheezed, pushing himself upright. "The legends speak of horrible monsters roaming the tunnels."

"Yeah. We met them," I answered.

Grohl looked me over, frowning, and Myria hurried to make introductions. "This is Aedan, he's a friend. He needs information about Flame, and Lukin. I think he could use our help." She smiled. "And I don't think I would have gotten this far without him. It's been an adventure."

Grohl shook his head as if to clear it, and coughed again. "I like the idea of helping someone who can fight like that. We can use all the strong allies we can get."

He nudged the other two men with the toe of his boot. "I'm glad you didn't kill them."

"I was trying to keep the noise down." I guess if these were Myria's friends, I didn't need to say that I was planning to finish them off once they were all down.

He merely raised an eyebrow. "All things have a purpose, all things have a plan." He coughed again. "Even if the plan is momentarily painful."

Slowly, they came to consciousness.

"Change of plan, boys. Let's head back up." The two younger men pushed up, faces dark with anger, but he waved their protests away.

"Myria brought us a new friend."

She looked away quickly. "Actually, it's not just Aedan. I'll be right back."

I watched as the two men stood, shoulders tense. Whatever the old one thought, they were still ready for a fight.

Something in my gut stirred. I didn't like this any more than they did.

"What are you doing down here," I asked him.

"None of your business," the darker haired one spat.

"Are you sure?" I growled, but in a moment, Myria had returned, leading Dayla by the halter.

Sweetie glared at the strangers from the cocoon of my coat, obviously not pleased about having her nap disrupted.

"Okay, now we're ready," Myria said. "Let's get back. I'm tired of running around in the dark."

Grohl laughed. "Have you run out of songs? Because it looks like you're looking for material to write your own saga!"

MYRIA

When we pushed past the crates that blocked the entrance of the tunnel from the rest of the cellar of Grohl's tavern, a lean woman with long blonde braids waited, knife drawn and ready.

"Myria!" exclaimed Helene. "What are you doing here?

"Your father thinks I'm gathering material for a new song." I hugged her, pleased beyond belief for a simple moment of friendship.

Then Dayla nudged me to get out of the way.

"We might have a problem getting her up the steps to go to the stable," I apologized.

"We'll be fine," Helene assured me. "Padsu is still convinced he's a born torwynn-whisperer. This will be a fine challenge for him."

Her oldest was ten, and obsessed with the herds that passed by the valleys surrounding Lukin in the summer months.

Then all thoughts of torwynn and boys fled my mind, as Aedan followed me into the cellar, carrying Sweetie nestled in his arms.

"Who, exactly, is that?" Helene whispered.

"She's not mine," I quickly answered. "We found her in a burned-out farm. She doesn't know what happened to her mother, other than bad people came."

Helene elbowed me. "I kinda figured. The girl would have been a hard secret to keep for as long as we've known each other. But who's the gentleman carrying her?"

My heart stopped, just for a minute. How to answer?

And would my answer now have to change all too soon?

"Aedan. He's a friend. He helped me get here." It wasn't enough. Not nearly enough. But it would have to do.

"I'm glad to see you're making such nice-looking friends," she teased, then approached Aedan and Sweetie. "Hi there," she said softly. "You look almost as old as my youngest. She's going to be five soon. Do you want to come play?"

Sweetie stayed pressed against Aedan's neck. "She

can stay with us, she's no bother," he said, patting her hair.

But Helene was clever with children. "I think I still have cookies left over from dinner upstairs. Should we go see?"

Sweetie held her arms out, and Helene took her up the stairs, softly promising treats and play time.

Aedan stepped over to me. "Are you sure the girl will be safe?" He sounded worried, and maybe even a little hurt at how easily Sweetie's loyalty had been bought.

"You mean, like she was with us?" I teased. Or meant to, but the look in his eyes betrayed how uncertain he was about all of this.

"I know how we got into the tunnels, but how did they know to come meet you?" The muscle in his jaw twitched. "Do you have a comm unit?"

"What? No!" I stepped back.

"I can answer that," Grohl answered. "This tavern's been around about as long as the castle. Longer, really. Miners used to stay here all the time when their shift was over. At least, that's what my father told me, what he remembers."

More men and women drifted down into the cellar, pulling crates and stools around to make a rough circle.

Most had brought something with them, a lantern, a tray of tankards, some cut-up bread. A bowl of hot water and bandages, that I used to start cleaning the bite on my leg from those stupid things.

Grohl took the nearest tankard, drank deeply. "There's bits and pieces of old tech around that we've never reported. We didn't know what it did, but it wasn't doing any harm where it was."

"Still doesn't explain how you knew the tunnel was there, what you were doing," Aedan growled. One of the men handed him a tankard of beer. He took it almost reflexively, without looking, without drinking.

"I found the tunnel when I was a boy," Grohl nodded in the direction of the passage, now covered with a stout wooden door, firmly locked. "I expect all of my kids did, in their time. And the grandkids. Never went far, because we'd all heard about the monsters that the warlords had left behind."

"But tonight," Tyf, the younger of the two men who'd come with Grohl, interrupted. "When I came down to get a new barrel, I saw a flashing red light. That old box on the shelf had started going crazy, blinking and beeping."

Grohl handed the box to Aedan, who turned it over in his hands. "Don't know what it is, but it seemed like maybe we should go check it out."

"A sensor receiver of some kind. Something must have triggered it when we were down there. Maybe motion activated in the upper tunnels. Maybe the shrieking of the not-tessas set it off."

"Not-tessas?" Tyf asked, looking between us. "If they weren't tessas, what were they?"

"I'll explain later," I said, finishing up with the bandage on my leg. "Hopefully, we'll never see them again."

"And while all of this is endlessly interesting," Grohl set his tankard down and leaned forward, fixing me with his stare. "Did you find it?"

Slowly, I slid the battered retrew case off my back, fingers catching in the cord that kept it shut.

I worried at it, back and forth. "I did." I looked around the room. "But somewhere, we must have a leak. I was attacked in Bitters."

"Impossible," snapped Grohl. "Everyone here has lost too much. They're committed."

"Maybe, but I've never been attacked in a town before." I risked a glance at Aedan. Storm clouds covered his face, his gaze that of a stranger. "Cutting back from the market, we were surrounded. I wouldn't have escaped if I'd been alone."

"They were after you, weren't they?" he asked, but from his tone, I could tell he knew the answer.

"Probably," I whispered.

"Did they get anything?" Grohl demanded, oblivious or uncaring to the tensions cutting across the cellar.

"No," I held the retrew case so tightly my fingers ached. "Luckily, I didn't have anything on me."

"You never said anything," Aedan said, his voice flat. "Never indicated that anything else was going on."

"I didn't have any choice," I spat back, guilt spurring my tongue faster. "I barely knew you. It wasn't your problem."

"It sure seemed like that at the time." He tilted his head to the side, as if seeing me for the first time. "Or did you just think it was useful to have a bodyguard in easy reach?"

I grabbed a tankard for myself. "You didn't seem terribly surprised that you'd be attacked in a dark alley. As far as I could tell, you always thought it was a possibility they knew what you were doing here."

I knew my argument sounded weak.

But it was true, wasn't it?

And it's not like he had been in any danger from it.

"It would've been useful to know," he insisted.

"How?" I fired back. "How would it have changed anything? Would you have done anything differently?"

Aedan shot me a hot look and I blushed, remembering some of the things he had done.

Would it have been different if I'd told him the truth from the beginning?

"It wasn't your problem," I repeated. "No matter what, you're going to complete your mission and then disappear back..." I caught myself, looking around the group.

That was between us, not them. If there was a leak, as I suspected, then I should be careful of Aedan's origins.

If Flame thought one hostage against the Emperor was a good idea, what would he think about the Emperor's quasi-brother-in-law?

I could keep a secret. Better than most.

"...disappear back where you came from," I finished weakly. "But we have to live with this."

"You could've trusted me," he growled.

I was too tired to fight anymore, too exhausted, too torn. "Like you trusted me with all your secrets?" I whispered.

His face shut down, and I felt sick to my stomach.

I didn't care about his secrets.

I didn't care what he was, or wasn't.

But I couldn't betray my friends.

"I couldn't tell you," I insisted finally. "Nobody speaks of this outside this room."

"Well, I'm here, in the damn room," Aedan snarled. "May as well speak, because I'm involved now, like it or not."

Grohl looked amused. "I think possibly that you are." His expression lightened. "Maybe you were always meant to be a part of our band. Did you ever think about that?"

From Aedan's stony look, I could guess his answer.

Grohl hastily moved on. "I believe Myria was about to explain the purpose of our band."

"Remember when you were talking down in the tunnels?" I started. "About bringing tech back? That it's important that we're not left with one person holding all the toys?"

Aedan nodded, waiting.

"It's not just the toys, it's the toymakers," I added.

He finally sipped from his tankard, but said nothing.

My own throat felt too tight to try drinking, so I just stared down into the liquid. "Flame is the last of the old warlords. Things had settled down, it'd been easier to trade, even across the desert and the wastelands. But about ten years ago, something changed."

Grohl picked up the story. "Not only do we suspect he's been hoarding, collecting remnants of tech, but he started arresting anyone who tinkers with building things. Anyone who gets too close to bringing back any kind of science, any sort of progress."

"You were right," I added. "No one erases progress. There are always notes, memories. We knew that everything was possible once." I bit my lip, wishing my words were making a difference. "We just want to have it again, make the future just a little brighter."

"I'm not here to interfere with the treaty," Aedan argued.

I snorted, finally took a drink. And then another. "Flame claims the arrests are to make sure that the treaty is followed. But no one ever hears again from the people he takes."

"There is a possible reason for that," Aedan said, face grim, "not a nice one, but nothing about Flame seems particularly nice."

"I know, but then three years ago, I got a message. From my sister, Lira."

Did I say I wished my words would make an impact on him, break through the expressionless mask he'd put on?

I took it back.

Aedan looked like I'd hit him. "You never mentioned a sister, either. Was that a deep dark secret, too?"

I was screwing this all up. But the only way out was to keep going.

"Sort of a secret. At least, the letter was. Lira was taken the year before I left home." I stopped, remembering her bright smile and how excited her eyes were as she coaxed one of her little projects to life. "She was beautiful, but more importantly, she was brilliant. She was curious about how everything worked, wanted to know how to make anything, everything, work better."

I leaned back, closed my eyes, remembering how it

had been before everything went so wrong. "Could she build a device to help with feeding the tessa so she didn't have to get up so early? Could she devise something to make washing the clothes easier? It was like an obsession with her. Lira couldn't help it."

And then I didn't want to remember. "Flame's soldiers came and took her away. We never saw her again."

Tyf spoke up. "They took my brother. He'd been studying how valars fly, how they can stay in the air for so long. Drawing them, dreaming of how they managed what seemed to be impossible."

An older woman said, "They took my daughter. She'd been trying to figure out a new paint for our farm. Something that would protect the wood better, make it stronger against the rain."

Round and round everyone spoke. Everyone had lost someone for the simple crime of being curious. Of wondering how things worked. Of wanting life to be better.

I continued. "Two years ago, someone passed me a note in a tavern. I don't know how they found me. I didn't ask them any questions. But it was her writing. Lira was alive. In Lukin. In the castle."

The others watched me eagerly, as they did every time I mentioned the letter. I'd been the only one to have news of my taken family. The only one who knew for certain they were alive.

Or at least, had been.

“She said at first it had been wonderful. That Flame had a laboratory set up where she could experiment, try anything she wanted. That he’d made it clear that anything she needed, she could have, just to ask. But she couldn’t leave.”

“What else?” Aedan asked softly. “There’s something else.

“She wanted me to send her love to our parents.” My hand stopped stroking the neck of the retrew and lay limp and lifeless in my lap. “There was no way to write back. No way to tell her they’d died less than a year after she’d been taken.”

The helpless anger that had washed over me reading her words all those months ago returned, spurred me on as it had over and over again. “And that’s what we’re doing here.” I glared at Aedan. “You can understand or not. Help or not. That’s up to you.”

AEDAN

"Great. That's what the problem is," I said, the words on autopilot. "But what do you think you're going to do about it? Start a revolution?"

I felt empty. Like I'd been torn up, ripped open, and Doc was putting me into one of the old healing pods.

Numb.

I've been an idiot to get involved. I knew the rules. Stick to the mission. Void, Myria had told me from the beginning, don't be an idiot.

So it was time to stop.

"We need to find out what's really going on in that castle," Myria said. "Flame has always been careful about who he hired to work inside. Usually he keeps a family member or two on tap to ensure their loyalty."

"Charming, but clever," I said. "Nice to have someone who thinks ahead."

"Honestly," Grohl interrupted, "that's how I would have described all of Flame's interactions up until about ten years ago." He took a long drink. "Sure, he was ruthless, but not unreasonable."

"So, something changed," I said. "Happens all the time. Maybe someone betrayed his trust, and he decided to buckle down." Myria refused to meet my stare. "What I still want to know is, how do you think any of this is going to help me?"

"Because I think we can get into the castle now," Myria answered, still not looking at me.

Slowly, she untied the retrew case and slid out the instrument.

Grohl kept talking. "My family has run this tavern since before the war. Half the workers that built the castle used to stay here, I'd expect."

Myria gently lifted the retrew out of the case. She didn't play it, just set it aside.

"One of the long-term residents was a builder. My grandfather said she was very clever, fixed things around the inn when she wasn't designing things at the castle."

Myria silently started picking at a seam in the lining of the retrew case, opening it a little, to reveal a hidden pocket.

"Two seasons ago, maybe three," Grohl continued, "Myria was late for her regular engagement in Lukin. Her problem was my luck. Another bard had taken her place at that inn, so she came here, looking for work."

Myria was halfway finished undoing the stitching now, and the fine, yellowing edges of what looked like paper peeked out.

"She'd heard about my younger brother who'd gone missing. Same story as the rest, really. Not much to add. But I started wondering. Wondering if there was a way to get in, look for those who'd been taken."

Myria picked up the story at that point, her long fingers stroking the scraps of paper covered in tiny writing as if they were an instrument.

"It took some doing to find her, the architect. Really, it was her children. She'd thought ahead, moved far away and changed her name before she had a family. She'd realized she'd have to be smart to avoid giving tiny hostages to fate. Or Flame."

The words were tinged with sadness, and I stubbornly kicked down the part of me that wanted to go brush her hair back, make it better.

"But people tell bards things, news and rumors, tidbits. And when I found her family, it turned out they'd had someone taken, as well. They were more than willing to help."

Myria tapped the stack of papers, then reached

across to hand them to Grohl. "Apparently, Flame's architect kept notes, and left them with her children as a sort of insurance."

Her smile of victory lit the cellar, brighter than any lantern. "There are secret passages all through the castle. And now we have the map."

The room exploded into noise and chaos.

Everyone wanted to see, wanted to get started, wanted to go and sneak through the castle and retrieve their family members immediately.

Tuning out the nonsense, I thought hard.

Myria was right, this could help me.

If the princess was in the castle.

If those passages weren't blocked up or monitored.

If I could find where Eladia was being kept.

If we could start soon enough.

My fingers itched for a look at the papers, but I stayed still, watching and thinking.

"We should leave right away," a tough-looking woman said. "We've spent too much time waiting."

"We should all go, gather everyone, storm the castle," shouted one of the younger men. "They'll never know what hit them!"

"Sure," I said quietly. "That sounds like a fine way to get yourself killed. Let me know when you're heading out, so I can avoid the mess, all right?"

Tyf glared at me. "What do you know about it?"

"I'm not exactly an expert in infiltration," I answered, because I wasn't. I couldn't pick up and put down a personality like Lorcan could.

Void, I hated that sort of work. And looking at Myria's hair, remembering the feel of it running through my fingers, I remembered why all over again.

"But I have actually managed to survive a few, which I'm guessing is more than most of the folks in this room. And the first part of the plan would be to confirm the information received with as small a party as possible to mitigate your risk."

"What does that even mean?" argued Tyf.

I tried not to roll my eyes. I probably wasn't successful.

Grohl answered for me. "He means we should send a scouting party, to see if we can get into the passages, check out how it looks, and then report back to the larger group to make a plan."

Grumbles and whoops filled the cellar as Grohl selected the members of the scouting party.

I didn't pay attention. Didn't care. I was going whether he selected me or not.

Their mission, their quest for their missing family members, that was their own business.

I had my own person to look for. And that was it.

"Things have probably changed in the castle since

the builder was here," Myria added. "It's not going to be as easy as it sounds."

"It doesn't sound easy at all," I said. "If Flame had those passages put in when the castle was built, what makes you think they're not guarded, or monitored, just like the mine tunnels were? You said he was clever. Don't you think he's put some thought into this?"

"There's only one entry point to the network of passages from the outer wall of the castle," Myria admitted. "The architect didn't say exactly where, just marked her notes with this symbol." She pointed at one of the pages. Three wavy lines. Maybe a clue. Maybe someone testing a pen. "Maybe a waterway, something with the drains? I think it looks like it's near the blacksmith's."

"Well then, no reason to get hot and bothered tonight," Grohl said, laughing at his own joke.

"The castle grounds are kept locked tight until the first bell. We may as well catch some sleep until then."

The rest of the room was silent, the reality of the situation sinking in. All of their months of waiting, hoping for something they could do.

And now the time had come.

"I'm going to catch a nap down here," I called over to Grohl.

He frowned, bushy gray eyebrows drawn together, as he looked between me and Myria.

"I've already sent one of the boys up to prepare one of the guestrooms for you and the singer. It's her usual room, just as she likes it."

Myria said nothing.

Grohl continued, trying to fill the awkward silence. "Didn't look like you have a lot of bags to take up, so that's a nice change from our usual visitors."

"I'll be fine down here," I insisted. "Wouldn't mind keeping an eye on that tunnel, even with the door locked. The things down there made me a bit nervous. Wouldn't want them sneaking up on me."

Myria climbed the stairs from the cellar without a backwards glance, and Grohl followed her, still looking worried.

But they left, and that was all that mattered.

As I lay in the dark and listened, I could hear the high-pitched whine of other hidden pieces of tech threading through the night air.

Maybe I should look for them. Maybe they would be useful.

But I kept straining my ears, listening for Myria's breathing in the room above.

MYRIA

I watched Sweetie sleeping, tumbled with the other children of the family as if she'd always known them, always been there.

"I'll ask around about her family in the morning," Helene had promised. "Someone will know who lived there, have some idea what happened."

And I knew she'd do it. Over the years, Grohl had slowly established a network, gathering information, rumors, anything.

Originally it had been to try to keep up with the flow of travelers, get information on weather, bands of outlaws.

But it had morphed, expanded. And now Helene could find out nearly anything in the region.

I wasn't really worried about Sweetie. She'd already shown she was far tougher than expected.

I couldn't imagine what tomorrow would bring. Would we even be able to get into the castle? Was all of this for nothing?

And once we were inside, what would we find?

Questions without answers swarmed in my mind.

In the silence of the sleeping tavern, I realized how much I'd become accustomed to Aedan's steady presence at my side.

In my arms.

But he'd made it very clear, and very public, that our relationship, whatever it had been, was over.

It *was* worth it. It had to be.

Getting that information was the only possible link to my sister.

And if he didn't understand it, well, we didn't have as much of a connection as I thought we did.

Finally, I gave up and went and sat by the banked fire in the kitchen, dozing into its glow, running the scarf through my hands. The purple and yellow blooms, just as bright as when I'd spotted it in the market.

At least something hadn't changed.

Tyf came down first and stoked the fire, then started the bread. "Too excited to sleep? I didn't think I kept my eyes closed for more than a minute, but suddenly, it was time to start the day."

"Something like that," I said.

One by one, the residents of the tavern drifted down. Helene led Sweetie into the room, still half-wrapped in Aedan's coat.

"Come here, honey." I held my arms out for her, and she climbed up. "Let's be all nice and snuggly by the fire."

Tyf brought over a piece of flatbread, still warm from the oven, and Sweetie and I took turns nibbling from it.

Helene's son, Padsu, bounced in. "Mom says you're leaving Dayla here for a few days, is that true? Can I try to train her?"

I laughed. "You can try, but I suspect she'll end up training you."

Grohl sat down with the architect's notes, so busy reading and re-reading that he paid no attention to his breakfast.

Finally, Aedan pushed open the door from the cellar, with eyes only for Sweetie.

"Mine!" she squealed, squirming down from my lap so quickly she almost tripped on the oversized coat.

He crouched down and she threw her pudgy arms around his neck. "Mine," she repeated contentedly.

For her, his face softened. "Glad you got a new word, kiddo."

She kissed his cheek and scrambled off his lap, wiggling out of the coat. "Yours." She thrust it at him.

He ran his hand over the fabric, and my breath caught in my throat.

I thought about the hours of travel I'd spent stitching it, idly thinking about him as we went, wondering what made him tick.

What had really brought him here.

Somehow, Aedan wearing it through the flood and the tunnels, everything had turned it into more than just a bit of camouflage, something to make him blend in.

It was foolish, I knew, but it felt like he was wearing a bit of my heart with that coat.

But instead of sliding the coat back on, he pulled it back around Sweetie, looping the sash four times around her waist before tying it. She giggled as the sleeves flopped and flailed over her far-too-short arms.

"Maybe it's yours now," he said softly. "Keep you warm. Keep you safe."

"But," I argued, "what if-"

"I'm done with hiding," he said flatly, the warmth that he had used when speaking to Sweetie gone, replaced by ice.

The mood of the kitchen changed, as people who weren't members of the scouting trip left, others arrived, shifting through gear, bringing bags with small lanterns, scraps of paper for notes.

Finally, it was just Grohl, Tyf, and a pair of young men who looked like they'd be good in a fight, but I wasn't exactly sure about their ability to keep a map in their mind.

And Aedan.

And me.

"What are you doing?" Aedan asked, when he realized I was staying.

"I'm part of the scouting party," I answered, trying to keep my tone level. "I've studied the maps. I'm the only one who has them memorized. We can't risk taking them with us."

Aedan took the papers from Grohl's hands, quickly flipped through them, and tossed them back down on the table. "Now there're two of us who have them memorized. You should stay."

Tyf scoffed. "No one can memorize anything that quickly."

Aedan turned, eyes flashing, and I hastily put a hand on his arm. "Now's not the time," I whispered.

"Take your hand off me," Aedan growled. But he left Tyf alone.

Finally, we were ready.

"Drift in, there's always a need for something at the blacksmith's, make some excuse to stick around and look for that symbol," Grohl said. "We'll pair up, make it more natural." And I would swear he grinned when he put me and Aedan together. "You have the experience, and she's seen the map. You go first, and we'll be ten, fifteen minutes behind you."

He handed a large iron stewpot to Aedan. "Take this with you, tell the blacksmith it needs to be mended."

Aedan looked at it doubtfully. "Does it?"

"Actually, yes. Just haven't gotten to it yet."

Anything else was lost as the chime of the first bell sounded through the city.

"It's time to go."

"Fine."

Aedan strode out through the tavern towards the street, and I scurried to keep up with him.

"We're supposed to be a pair," I whispered, taking his hand, hating how his muscles tensed at my touch. "Look, I know you're angry with me. But you don't even know where the blacksmith's is, do you?"

Aedan just pointed with the stewpot.

And to my annoyance, he was right.

"How could you possibly know that?"

"Listened. A smithy isn't exactly the quietest of places."

Of course.

The streets were already full, despite the early hour. We joined the throng of people flowing through the castle gates, merchants and workers, buyers and sellers, all ready to get on with the day.

As we passed through, I tugged Aedan to the right.

"You might be able to hear the hammer," I said, "but the smithy is in the back of the castle. We'll have to take the path around. Come on."

He didn't argue, and we made our way slowly through the crowd that had formed outside the smithy.

Joining the line to give our work to the blacksmith's assistant, I peered around, trying to find anything that might possibly be a clue to a secret door.

The smithy was centered against the back wall of the castle, huge fireplaces burning along the wall, and three large anvils in constant, deafening use. The front was open, the sides enclosed with metal, lined with ceiling-high stacks of firewood.

But unsurprisingly, nothing that looked like a secret door.

Once we reached the front of the line, Aedan shoved the pot at the burly young man. "Pot needs to be fixed," he said flatly.

The assistant glared at him and my heart sank.

"Oh goodness, honey," I cooed at Aedan, pinching his arm sharply. "He'll think you have no manners at all."

Turning my brightest smile on the assistant, I rolled my eyes at Aedan. "My husband hit his head on the doorway this morning, and ever since he's been such a grumpy bear."

Aedan growled, and I pinched him again, turning back to the assistant.

"I'm sure a big, strong man like you knows what it's like to be just too large for your surroundings, right?"

With a grin and a leer, the assistant took the pot and waved us along. "Should be ready later today," he said, then turned to the next person in line.

"What the hell was that?" Aedan snarled when we'd barely passed out of earshot.

"That was me making sure we made it through the very first hurdle," I shot back. "I know you said you weren't an expert in infiltration, but please, tell me how you survived any missions acting like that. Because I'm just not seeing it."

He didn't answer, which left me to drift through the crowd, smiling and chatting with people while he stayed a silent lump.

"So good to see you again!" I said for the fourteenth time. "Yes, I'm over at Grohl's tavern for a while. Come by and we'll have a good gossip."

"How do you know all these people?" he muttered after the woman left.

"I'm a bard," I sighed. "I travel through all the towns. Knowing people is my business." I elbowed him, just a little. "Although, the way a few of the women were batting their lashes, they'd like to get to know you quite a bit better, as well."

"Don't think so," he answered, but he elbowed me back. Just a little. Just enough to make me think that maybe we could at least be friends.

Even if the chance for something more had been lost.

We wandered around the side of the smithy, away from the crowd, looking for anything out of the ordinary.

"Why would you put a forge right next to a building?" I wondered. "I know I'm not an architect, but it seems like a recipe for disaster, even if it is all made of stone."

"There's a tickle in my head," Aedan mused. "Something on one of the vids Doc had us watch."

"Who's Doc?" I asked.

"The mad scientist we call mother," he answered absently. "She has a thing about making sure we learned everything that past human societies did, or built. Like I said, no one erases progress. And once something is discovered, even if it's lost, humans will figure it out again and again."

I studied the castle wall before us, mind reeling as I tried to put together the pieces he'd thrown out so casually.

Why did he call a mad scientist mother? And who

was 'we'?

The barest movement caught my attention, a flash of teal scampering across the ground.

A tiny skelic was running back and forth with twigs, probably building her nest. I kept watching, glad of the chance to give my mind a break from all the complications.

Except…

"That's strange," I pulled Aedan's arm to bring him back from whatever place in the past his mind had gone, rummaging for memories. "Look at that," I pointed to the skelic. "Watch where she's going."

"How do you know it's a she?" he argued. "And, besides, one more strange creature, doing strange things…"

He trailed off, and I knew he'd seen it.

The back wall of the castle to the right of the forge looked like a solid expanse, heavy, unbroken.

The skelic had run right through it. Not through a tiny crack, or down a hole, just through the wall at an angle, like nothing was there.

She'd been carrying a twig in her mouth, as long as she was. There wasn't a crack that size.

"Some sort of hologram?" Aedan wondered. Looking around to check if anyone was paying us special attention, we moved closer to the wall.

I reached forward, but he pulled me back to his side.

"Careful. If there's a hologram covering an opening, there could be anything else mixed up with it. Lasers, or a pit on the other side, guards, anything."

I sighed. "The skelic has been running back and forth for minutes now. She doesn't seem to have fallen into a pit, or been fried by a laser."

By that time, Grohl, Tyf and the two fighters had joined us. I pointed at the taller of the two. "Do me a favor? Follow that skelic."

He looked at Grohl, looked at the skelic, and shrugged. "Okay."

Definitely not who I was putting in charge of map making.

We all watched as he stepped up to the wall, paused to wait for the flash of teal to pass his feet, and took another step.

I blinked.

I could still see him. And the wall.

But suddenly, it was as if my vision had shifted, as if I could see that it wasn't a solid wall at all.

An opening split the wall into two, and another one, of the exact size and shape of stone, sat behind the false wall, creating the illusion.

I hurried to his side, Aedan behind me.

There was a narrow passageway, running towards the forge.

And on the interior wall, clearly marked, was the symbol again.

"This has to be it!"

I pulled back, thinking, and we wandered away from the opening, back towards the forge.

"We could use a distraction," I muttered. "Something to make sure we're not spotted disappearing down there."

Aedan didn't answer, just reached out. With a powerful twist, he yanked out a log from the stack of firewood.

Nothing happened.

And then the entire wall of wood shifted, tilted, and tipped, finally rolling out into the courtyard, tumbling into the crowd.

I could only stare at him.

"Nobody's watching us now, are they?" he said flatly. "Let's get going."

AEDAN

Our party slid behind the false wall, following the narrow passage toward the forge. Right before it would have led into the fireplaces, it made a sharp turn towards the castle, ending in a shallow alcove.

"Maybe you don't know what you're doing, bard," Tyf sneered.

"She knows a damn sight more than you do," I snarled, annoyed at his presumption.

Myria was right. In my gut, I knew it. Examining the dead end in front of us, there was a faint vertical crack.

And to the side of it, the symbol again, etched into the stone.

I tapped it to make my point, then shoved at the crack and felt it give, just a bit.

"It's just stuck," I said. "Hold on."

I wedged my fingers in the crack and forced it back, grateful for the hubbub of the crowd that covered up the mighty screech of a mechanism long fallen out of use.

The air blasted over us, hot and dry.

"Hypocaust," I blurted. "Ancient Terrans used them to warm buildings, heated air and let it rise throughout the structure. It's not water, the symbol is for air."

Myria looked at me with a raised eyebrow. "What can I say. Doc's something of a history freak."

"Will this lead us into the rest of the castle?" Grohl asked, peering down the corridor.

"To allow the air to heat the building, we should find vents leading from this area all throughout the building," I mused. "This must be some sort of maintenance access."

"But is it safe?" Tyf complained. "Why aren't there guards here?"

Despite the heat that had initially overwhelmed my sense of smell, I still felt safe that our motley party was alone.

"Look at the dust on the floor. It's not just that that door in the wall hasn't been opened, no one's been here in years."

"I wouldn't come here if I didn't have to," the darker of the pair of fighters commented. "Too hot."

"I kinda like it," Myria answered. "What?" she fussed when I looked askance at her. "I hate being cold."

"I'll keep that in mind," I commented as we went deeper into the room, then regretted my words.

I didn't need to keep anything in mind anymore. Not about her.

We followed the passage away from the heat, our way dimly lit by air shafts high above. Finally, we came to another door, this one quite ordinary. I listened for any movement on the other side, footsteps, conversations, machinery.

Nothing.

"Let's keep going," I waved the party through, waiting for everyone to pass. "What are you waiting for?" I motioned for Tyf to rejoin the group. He stood staring around him, as if trying to memorize everything.

"Now where do we go?" Grohl asked. The corridor the last door had opened onto branched off in either direction. "Are there any more of those helpful symbols?"

We scattered to search, but found nothing.

"I think we should go back," said the chatty fighter, who's name I still hadn't bothered to learn. "This is just a scouting trip, right? Well, we found our way in. We should tell the others."

He did have a point. It would be the safe thing to do. Maybe even the smart thing.

But I wasn't leaving. Not this close to my goal.

"Do you see our families anywhere?" Myria snapped. "No? Then I don't think we're done scouting."

She looked at me, confident I'd have an answer. "Where do you think we should start?"

"Your sister said she was in some kind of a lab or workshop," I mused. "From what I know about scientists and their experiments, anyone, even only partially sane, would want to set that away from the main living quarters."

Myria nodded, thankfully not asking too many questions about that. "It's not like Flame could have built a dungeon here, between the mines below and this place that must run underneath the entire building. There's just no room."

"What about the towers?" Grohl asked.

I thought about where we'd currently be located in the castle, rotated the map in my mind. "Closest tower would be this way," I pointed down one branch of the corridor.

"How do you know that?" the second fighter grumbled.

Myria smothered a laugh. "I always ask him that, but

he never has a good answer." She followed me. "Just trust him."

The passageway ended with a smaller door, opening to a tight, circular staircase that rose high overhead.

"This must run all the way through the middle of the tower," Grohl muttered to himself. "It would lead into each of the rooms. Wonder if I could do something like this at the inn?"

We started up the narrow stairs. I led the way, with Myria right behind me, followed by the dark-haired fighter, then Grohl, then the other fighter, and Tyf guarding the rear.

At the first landing, we stopped.

"You're right," Myria whispered. "There's a wooden grate here, but also…" her hand knocked away layers of dust to reveal the outline of a door. She looked at me, frowning. "Why would they put a full-sized door here? You wouldn't want to push that much hot air into a room at once, would you?"

"You said Flame was clever," I answered. "He ended up with central heating, spy holes, and hidden doors all throughout the castle, all in one go. That's clever and practical."

But despite all of us peering through the grate, we discovered nothing more interesting than crates and sacks of food stores in the room before us.

"Let's keep going," Myria said. "Maybe they're all

just higher up in the tower. Like you said, maybe they put the workshop as far away from the main level as possible. Maybe they're just on the next floor."

But they weren't.

Not in that tower, nor in the next.

We did find the armory. Interesting to me, and possibly useful if necessary, but no kidnapped family members, and no princess.

As we made our way back down to the base of the second tower, I noticed Myria and Grohl were fading a bit, steps dragging.

"Why don't you go back to the tavern, wait for me there?" I offered. "You might like the heat, but you're not used to it. I promise to let you know if I find anything."

Myria looked up at me, her face filthy with dust and her hair tangled and bedraggled where it had fallen out of her braid. And still beautiful.

"I can't," she said. "Thank you. I know you'd tell me. But I can't give up now, not when it feels like we're so close."

I hadn't really expected her to agree.

And then I looked at the rest of the group. "Where in all the Void is Tyf?"

Grohl quickly turned around, searching the small space. "Maybe he heard your offer, went ahead and headed back to the tavern?"

Possible. He did seem like the sort to give up at the first opportunity.

"But you two are staying with me!" Grohl thumped the chests of the two fighters. "And I'm staying here.

"Yes, sir," they sighed.

Wearily, hot and sweaty, we began the ascent of the third tower.

Nothing on the first level, or the second.

The third floor housed a library, a vast collection of old-style books that I bet would be worth a fortune.

And on the fourth level, we finally found someone.

An old man, snow white hair still thick, sat looking out the tower window, the walls around him draped with tapestries woven in the black and orange of Flame.

Once-broad shoulders looked shrunken and bowed, and deep lines scored the side of his face that was turned to the grate. A heavy chain of office hung around his neck.

For a moment, I thought his eyes caught mine as I stepped back, but he turned toward the window.

I switched places with Myria so she could have a clearer view.

"Anyone you know?" I whispered.

She shook her head and was about to make room for Grohl to look when a woman entered the room.

From the back, all I could see was her deep green, belted dress made of plain, sturdy looking fabric, similar to what Myria had shown me in the market back at Bitters. Long silver braids spilled down her back, clasped with twisted golden bands.

She carried a tray with two steaming mugs that she carefully placed on the table by the old man's elbow.

"My dear," he said, "you shouldn't be fussing over me like that."

She turned away from the window, and reality shifted, then recentered.

His 'dear' was my missing princess.

Out of the confines of her court regalia, she looked softer, happier. Time had only made her more beautiful. Face bare of the elaborate makeup she'd worn in the official portrait Vandalar had shown me, her only jewelry was a short necklace of beaten gold disks that highlighted the length of her neck.

"You know I'm always grateful for your company," the old man said as he took her hand and kissed the tips of her fingers. "But if you don't mind, I'd like you to step behind my chair, just for a minute."

"You're being ridiculous, Jomu," she smiled. "But I rather like indulging you. Feels like we're making up for lost time."

Once she had moved, the old man slowly pulled himself upright, leaning heavily on a thick wooden cane, the end tipped with metal.

He looked straight across the room, and this time there was no mistake when he met my gaze.

"You've come all this way, you may as well come in."

Myria looked up at me, shocked silent.

I shrugged. "It's one old man. He hasn't seen you yet, but I need to go in there."

She didn't answer, but slipped her hand in mine.

The secret door swung open with a gentle push, and together, we stepped into the room.

Nadira probably would have suggested that I kneel. Granny Z would have looked for something to plunder.

A short bow seemed like a reasonable compromise.

"Your Highness, we received word that you'd been kidnapped. I've come to rescue you."

With a glance, I could tell that she knew where I was from, if not exactly what I was.

The easy smile she'd worn for her captor steeled into an icy mask. "Does it look to you like I need rescuing? Does it look like I'm in chains, miserable, starving?"

She stalked out from behind the chair like an angry lioness, and I took a half-step back.

"What kind of idiot has my brother sent after me this time?"

Having met my share of Imperial troopers, I didn't feel that insulted, at least not on their behalf.

A little bit stung that she'd lumped me in with them, but she wasn't to know.

"Your Highness, your brother didn't send me. Vandalar did. Back at the Hub..."

I trailed off.

There was no good way to say this, was there?

I had focused so much on finding her, and not really thought about how to break the news.

Her brother was, if not dying, close enough to it that he wanted to abdicate.

"It's time. Vandalar's coronation is soon. If I don't return with you, he'll be forced to come with the fleet. Their priority would be to locate you, with no regard for the local populace."

"Oh." Eladia's face paled and she staggered just a bit.

The old man glared at me and helped her to the chair that he had recently vacated.

"You're an asshole, boy, anyone ever tell you that?"

"Many times, sir."

"I'll go," the princess said. "If for no other reason than to tell that nephew of mine that I haven't been kidnapped, and that I have the right to go where I please." She rested her head on the old man's arm. "And where I please is right here."

"Maybe you should have told him that before you left," I said mildly. "Would have saved us all a lot of headaches."

A thought struck me. "But, if you're here of your own free will, why did the Emperor receive a ransom note from Flame?"

The princess and the old man stared at each other.

"Ransom note," the old man shook his head. "Nonsense. Just that bastard trying to stir things up again."

"Nonsense or not, Vandalar has a very detailed, very extensive demand for weapons, coming from someone calling themselves Flame."

I turned to face him fully. "I assume that would be you?"

The man laughed. "Once upon a time, sure. Young man's folly and pride, taking a moniker like that." He shook his head. "It's a hard name to live up to, doesn't really lend itself to a peaceful retirement. Once I decided I wanted to stay and get some rest, catch up with my books, I chose one of my captains to pick up the mantle."

He chuckled. "It was nice to be plain old Jomu for these last few years. And then when I got my lovely Ellie's message, I knew I'd made the right choice."

Ellie? I blinked, as reality seemed to shift around me again. Right. Eladia.

"I know you have responsibilities here." The Princess Eladia, apparently also known as Ellie, reached out to hold Flame's hand.

Not Flame Jomu. It made as much sense as anything else right now.

"But would you consider coming back with me? As my guest. It sounds like there will be quite a lot of change soon. The event itself is sure to be stuffy, but the food is usually quite good. And it might make up for your treatment the last time you came to the capital." Princess Eladia extended an invitation.

"I would be honored to go anywhere you wish," he beamed down at her, then turned to glare at me. "And get to the bottom of this ransom nonsense."

"Fine with me," I said. "My part in all this is over."

I tugged at the seam of my shirt, the too-well-fitting, too-perfect shirt that Myria had insisted gave me away, made me stick out as not from around these parts.

She was right, I was sure. But there were reasons I couldn't do without it.

A thin piece of dull gray metal slowly emerged from the fabric.

Jomu stepped back in front of the princess, cane held out like a cudgel.

"What the hell is that, boy?" he asked warily.

"Just a burstcomm," I answered, too sick and tired of this whole mission to even start to take offense. "Let them know it's time to pick her up."

And get me off this planet, I said to myself, get my head back on straight.

It was one of Doc's newest toys, the reinforced structure difficult for even one of her Wolves to break.

But in an instant, I had it snapped, the pre-recorded message zipping away to the ships waiting above.

"They should be here by the morning," I told Eladia. "Vandalar isn't a bad guy. Gets on my nerves, but really, most people do."

She smiled slightly. "Is he still putting on that hapless idiot act?"

"Right, you've met him." I pushed my hair back and thought about how long ago that conversation seemed now. "But the thing is, he's not an idiot, and he's not cruel, either. Talk to him after the coronation. He's not going to put up a fuss about you going wherever makes you happy."

"And while we're waiting for the ship," I said as turned to Jomu, "maybe you can give the rest of these folks some answers about their families. The whole kidnapping thing seems to have gotten out of hand."

I turned to Myria, ready to force the old man to listen to her, to find her sister.

But Myria was gone.

MYRIA

Kaljak's hand pressed tightly over my mouth and his other arm wrapped around me, pinning my arms to my sides, as he dragged me backwards from the room.

"Not a peep, my little singer," he whispered, and a sharp prick at my neck made my eyes water. "My friend here isn't really a fan of yours."

I glanced around wildly to find Tyf pressed against my side, a long knife held at my throat. "You'll hold still and stay quiet, won't you?"

"Come on," Kaljak ordered, and between the two of them, they quickly lifted me into the air, Tyf holding my feet while he backed down the stairs and Kaljak keeping my back pressed against his chest.

Despite my struggles, they were too big, too strong.

But they wouldn't be for Aedan, my treacherous brain reminded me.

Except, he wasn't here. He'd found his princess. He'd made it clear that was his only priority now.

I was on my own.

The short hallway turned into a grand zigzagging staircase, but unlike the tiny circular one, this part of the castle was cold. The chill in the air was only part of the reason for the ice running through my veins.

Kaljak chuckled as he held me tightly. "You kept running away and running away. It made me very angry, you know. But finally, you ran straight to me."

Tyf grumbled and adjusted his hold on my feet as they went past another landing, down another level. "You wouldn't have known about her being here if I hadn't told you. Or about those hidden tunnels."

"Of course, of course. You did a great job." I couldn't see Kaljak's face from my position, but insincerity dripped from his voice. "You've always been a valued asset, a good friend to the cause."

Maybe Aedan was right. Tyf was an idiot. He didn't seem to notice the tone, just soaked in the praise he so obviously craved.

"Now that you have her, what are you going to do with her?" Tyf grinned, eyes alight with menace.

A shiver of fear ran through me. They weren't even

bothering to keep their voices down, didn't care who heard them.

Kaljak had grabbed me before I heard any explanations, but back in the tower room, I'd thought the old man must be Flame, must be in charge.

And I'd spent years learning to size up people on sight. Whatever other crimes he'd committed, the warlord seemed to respect Aedan, or at least, might be willing to work with him.

But if that wasn't the case, if the old man wasn't in charge of the castle, I was in real trouble.

"I have lots of ideas," Kaljak said as they exited the tower into a long corridor, one side punctuated by graceful pointed arches leading to an interior courtyard.

A fountain burbled in the middle of a garden, and all in all, it was an incongruous place to be kidnapped.

If I was on my own, I had to remember where I was taken, what the path was to escape.

"I want her." Kaljak held me even tighter, and I tried not to gag against his hand. I could feel exactly how much he wanted me. "But I want those weapons more. The brute who said he was her husband, I doubt he really cares about that shriveled old crone, princess or not." He squeezed my waist. "He'll trade the Imperial bitch back to me in exchange for this one."

"But maybe we can have some fun first," Tyf said.

Like hell.

I drew my knees up slightly, just enough for leverage, then kicked out the heels of my boots, catching Tyf in the chest.

As he stumbled back, my feet slammed to a clatter on the floor.

I twisted to break Kaljak's grip on me and managed to get a step away, but before I could get any further, Tyf's knife was back at my neck. "Stupid move, bard," he snarled. "You're not untouchable here."

"I can walk," I insisted, chin held high.

As we went deeper into the castle, I let my hand trail against the wall.

Unlike the heating tunnels, these were clean, well-polished. There would be no lovely trail through the dust to lead searchers to me.

But maybe, just maybe, his senses were good enough that Aedan might be able to pick up my scent.

I held onto that hope. Until I came up with a better plan, it was all I had.

Guards filled the hallways here, all in the orange and black tabards. And they all bowed to Kaljak.

A prick of pain as my nails bit into my palms. That wasn't good.

Kaljak took my arm, drawing me close as if we were a couple out for a stroll, if you ignored the knife now poking into my side.

"The old man had gathered all those bits of technology before. All the things that had been left behind. And he did nothing with them!" His voice was outraged. "He created that damnable peace with the other old men, instead of pressing his advantage, conquering the whole region."

"Flame didn't *let* the peace happen," I forced out. "Everyone was tired of the fighting, of the dying. Everyone wanted peace."

"But at what cost?" Kaljak snapped. "What did we get out of it? This?" He waved at the stone corridor as we mounted another set of stairs. "The rest of the universe is sprawled among the stars and we are trapped on a ball of mud. All because of a peace that none of us living here and now agreed to."

Another tower, I hoped, but it didn't seem right. We'd already passed an arch that led to another set of zigzag stairs.

These steps led to a broad double door set into the middle of a wall. More guards were stationed here, at the top and the bottom of the stairs, and again at either side of the door.

He led me up, ignoring the bowing guards, Tyf at our heels, the dagger still at my back.

"So you want to start another war? How is that going to help anything?" I argued.

The guards stepped aside smartly as Kaljak swung

open the door.

We stepped through to a short balcony, looking over a vast room filled with tables, people, and things I didn't even know how to explain spread before me.

Kaljak smiled proudly, surveying his domain. "No, I want to give us back our future." The smile became fixed, the eyes hard. "Whatever it takes."

This time, Aedan had been wrong.

The workshop wasn't in the tower. I tried to map the castle in my mind, and decided this room must have been built after the original construction, pushing out to the side we didn't take on our way to the forge. The path everyone took would have avoided this entire area.

Aedan most definitely had been wrong about the tower.

I didn't know why my mind was so hung up on that one fact as I gazed across the room.

Probably because it was the one fact that I could easily understand.

The room stretched out below us, clusters of people grouped around long tables, some with attached benches, some not.

In one corner, six men and women worked on an oddly shaped metal sculpture with protrusions and grooves running through it and smoke sputtering out.

"An internal combustion engine," Kaljak said. "An

antique to the rest of the Empire, but it would revolutionize things here. Even if we don't use it for long, we need to have a better grasp of the basic principles."

Another group endlessly adjusted a tray filled with lights and crystals, a third circled around a stack of glassware filled with brightly colored bubbly liquids.

Everywhere I looked, people were doing absolutely unimaginable, incredible things. And all around the perimeter of the room, more guards stood watch, silent and ready.

"It's amazing," I gasped. "I don't even know what they're all doing, but I know it's something amazing."

Kaljak smiled, and for a moment he was actually handsome.

"I knew you'd understand." He squeezed my arm, excited. "This is our future, waiting for us."

I shook my head, reluctant to break the spell. "It is amazing, really. But how many of these people wanted to be here? How many of them did you take from their homes?"

He waved the truth away like inconvenient smoke.

"How many people would be killed each year because we don't have access to proper technology? Medicines? Agricultural techniques?" His eyes shone even brighter. "All of those advances were lost to us because of the peace."

My arm throbbed as his grip became tighter. Tyf

stepped to my other side, knife lowered as he gazed across the floor with the same hungry, acquisitive look. But there was no escape.

Not yet.

"You tell me, which is worse? Encouraging a few dozen people to give up their homes and families, make a better technology so we all have a better way of life, so our children can reclaim their rightful place in the stars?" Kaljak dragged me down the short flight of steps from the observation deck. "Or should I let us continue to be abandoned to the stone ages?"

As we descended, a man at the table closest to us moved, and I could see the chains. A quick glance at the rest of the tables told me the truth. Every worker down there wore a broad belt with a length of chain tethering it to a metal hoop in the middle of their assigned table. Some wore additional chains on their wrists, others on their ankles.

As we reached the bottom of the stairs, an explosion ripped through the far side of the room. Shouts cut the air, accompanied by the crackle of broken glass and the heavy steps of guards running towards the noise.

Kaljak shoved me at Tyf. "Watch her. Carefully," he snarled, and strode off down the center aisle to deal with whatever had happened.

"Why don't you just sit here and be quiet, little bird?" Tyf leered. "I'm sure we can find more interesting activities when he comes back. He might be willing to trade you for the princess, but he's never said what sort of shape you'd be in." The knife flicked at my throat again, and I stumbled back, hand pressed against my neck.

I half sat, half collapsed on the long wooden bench closest to me and tried to still the shaking of my hands.

This was a room filled with weapons, if I only knew how to use them. I examined the items strewn all over the bench, trying to make sense of the jumble of pots in front of me. But I didn't recognize anything. Maybe one of the jars would be heavy enough on its own to throw?

But how would I get past the guards?

Something tickled at the back of my mind. A scent. The sort of thing I'd laughed at when Aedan paid attention to it.

Smoke.

Looking up, I met the eyes of the woman chained to the table across from me. Her face was bruised, her hair singed. And she looked wild with worry.

Time for one of Aedan's hunches.

"This is gonna sound crazy," I whispered. "Are you the mother of a little girl, brown hair, big eyes, likes pretty soft things?"

Her chains rattled as she covered her mouth quickly and her eyes shone with tears.

"Heidy?" she whispered. "You found Heidy? Is she

safe? Where is she?"

"If you lived in a farmhouse half a day's ride west of Lukin, we've got her." I whispered back.

The woman's eyes flew around the room frantically.

"No, no," I tried to reassure her. "Not here, she's safe, with friends."

The woman's shoulders shook with silent sobs and I looked away, embarrassed to be watching her emotion.

"It's nice to have a real name for her," I said to the air. "We've just been calling her Sweetie. She said that was her name."

The woman sniffled, and a smile broke through. "I guess it's what I call her enough that she's forgotten she has another name," she said weakly.

"And she's fine. She had a good night's sleep and a full belly. Maybe too many cookies," I promised. "She'll be so happy to see you."

"I don't think that's going to happen any time soon," the woman said dejectedly, looking down at her chains.

"From what I've heard from the others when I was taken to the dorms, no one leaves. Not after they start working for the 'grand vision' of that lunatic, Flame." Her mouth twisted scornfully. "You can't force progress like this. None of us want to follow the same path as the ancients. We have our own world we want to learn about. Sure, Imperial technology would be nice, but this isn't the right way to advance."

I leaned over the table to her. “Here’s another oddness to add to the pile,” I whispered. “I don’t think that’s really Flame. He’s too young, for one thing.”

Sweetie’s mother shrugged. “What difference does it make? He’s the one in control of the guards.”

“It matters,” I insisted. “There’s more going on than he knows or can control, guards or not.”

Was I trying to bring her spirits up, or my own?

“All right,” I pointed to the jars and vials on the table. “Tell me what all this stuff is. Something here could get us out, we just have to think.”

But before I could get any further, Kaljak was back.

“I don't know where we're going to get more beakers of that size,” he muttered. “I'll need to find somebody working on better glass production techniques.”

He pulled me along with him as we passed workbench after workbench. Everyone kept their eyes down and their hands busy.

“You see the problem, don't you, restarting everything from scratch,” Kaljak looked more irritated than anything. “I know what we need to do, but we don't have the tools to get there so we have to build those. But we don't even have the tools to build those, and on and on it goes.”

Taking a deep breath, I calmed my heartbeat, just as

if it was any other performance. “I think your idea is brilliant.”

He stopped, looked sideways at me. “You do?”

“I'm not saying I agree with how you're going about it,” I clarified. “But you're right, we do need to find a better future.”

Words were my weapons. They always had been, they always would be.

They were my tools, and with the words, maybe I could save myself, and set the others free, as well.

But that depended on being able to reach him.

“How else do you think this should work?” he spat. “Look around. These people don't want to be here. They want to idly study whatever catches their fancy, poke around the edges of some other fascinating property in their spare time.” His scorn was palpable. “They don't have a vision, directive.”

I had to reach him, somehow. “It’s impressive, what you’re trying to do. How did the vision come to you?”

Kaljak scoffed. “I saw the pieces of scraps the old man had confiscated, locked away. His library, where old-timers had frantically written paper manuals, notes and scraps of information from devices that would never work again.” He grabbed my upper arms tightly. “They wanted us to find the way back to the future!” He shook me slightly in his agitation. “Can't you see that? They left us a roadmap.”

"You're hurting me," I said softly.

But he didn't seem to hear.

"The old man didn't have the stomach for it," he said, then finally released me.

Stumbling back, a steadying arm reached for me, held me up for just a moment. I looked up to thank the stranger and was shocked to realize it wasn't a stranger at all.

"Edrel!" I cried out, then glared at Kaljak. "What is he doing here?"

"You couldn't possibly think I would let someone who was experimenting with that kind of machinery go ungathered? Besides," he smiled again, and it was no longer handsome, but twisted, mad. "I had a score to settle with him." He stepped towards me. "Just like I do with you."

Kaljak ran a finger down my cheek, and I knew I'd lost, my attempt to reach him failed.

"I've sent my men up to the tower. I don't need the old man anymore. But I do want your husband. Or is he, really?"

But whatever his plans were, they were silenced when a roar of rage echoed through the room.

"What was that?" Edrel whispered behind me.

Kaljak's lips pressed into a fine line, so I answered for him.

"I think my husband has noticed that I'm missing."

AEDAN

"Where did she go?" I demanded of Grohl.

He shook his head, just as lost as I was. "I didn't see anything. I was, well, watching all of this," he waved a hand between me and the warlord and the princess.

Fair enough.

Part of me knew I couldn't blame him, but the rest of me wanted to know where Myria was.

Needed to know.

I looked at the two fighters. They were as blank as ever.

The door from Jomu's quarters to the hall was partially open.

Had it been that way when we came in through the passageway?

I raced out.

No Myria.

But there on the landing was a drop of blood.

Hers.

A roar that came from the depths of my soul shook the walls around me.

"Wait!" called out Jomu. "Take this."

He jerked the medallion from around his throat and tossed it to me.

"Any of the men who are truly loyal to me should obey you."

"If they're not," I didn't wait for him to finish. "Anyone who stands between me and my mate will regret it."

Jomu nodded his understanding. "Try to give them a chance to surrender, if it's not too much trouble."

"You," I barked at the fighters that had guarded Grohl. "Make sure no one comes near the princess."

They looked confused, but Grohl nodded. "We'll take care of her."

And I was off.

It didn't matter anymore what Myria had done, or what'd she'd said or hadn't said.

Tearing down the stairs, I met two of the guards running up, swords drawn.

I wanted to rip their throats out, but on the off

chance they could turn into allies, I held up the medallion and gave them a moment to choose.

They didn't stop. I was all right with that.

I left their bodies behind me as I went down to the next level.

Two more rushed to meet me. Of those, one stopped, lowering his sword at the sight of the medallion.

His companion ran him through, then turned to me. The first guard was quickly avenged.

"Myria," I shouted, my voice echoing down the hall.

No answer, just the pounding feet of more troops approaching.

Vandalar would say my duty was to the princess.

But I knew better.

At the bottom of the stairs, I turned, searching for clues. But all I found were more guards.

This time, both of them stopped at the sight of the medallion. They even came to attention.

"One of you, go to the tower and guard Jomu now," I commanded. Whatever was happening in this place, the tension was thick in the air, a storm ready to break. "You, where would I find the new commander, the one who calls himself Flame?"

"He's probably in the laboratory," the guard answered.

"Show me the way, quickly."

The closer we got to the laboratory, the more I was sure that was where Myria had been taken. Her scent filled the air.

Another pair of guards, the first dispensed with quickly, the next either loyal or smart enough to see where their best chance of survival lay.

Bursting through the door, a familiar sight lay before me, but warped, distorted.

Instead of coated scientists happily working on their experiments, row after row of prisoners labored for a madman, chained and beaten.

And I would deal with it later. There was only room for one thought in my head now.

Get Myria. Make sure she was safe.

I leapt over the railing of the viewing platform to land on one of the tables below.

A woman with a bruised face pointed towards the far end of the hall.

"He took her that way, hurry."

I nodded my thanks and ran, as the loyal guards hurried behind, then froze as her gasp cut the air.

Jomu had mentioned the young captain who'd taken on the mantle of Flame.

The one who'd been harassing Myria from the beginning.

The one whose scent I had caught at the burned farmhouse.

Kaljak.

Myria stood at the far end of the room, Kaljak holding her upper arm tightly, and Tyf, the traitor, pressing a knife to her throat.

As I watched, a drop of blood fell, staining the garden of her scarf.

"Are you all right?" I asked Myria.

"I will be," she said and smiled. "Try to keep the incidental damage down, would you?"

It was a minor thing, but knowing that she had the utmost faith in my ability to save her spurred me on.

Sure, we had some stuff to figure out. But it didn't matter what she had or hadn't done, what secrets she'd kept. Or that I'd kept.

We'd work it out, that was certain.

The other fact that was certain was that I was going to kill the trash who had laid hands on her.

I took a step towards her, and Tyf pressed the knife harder against her skin. She stayed silent this time, but her widened eyes spoke volumes.

The entire hall fell quiet, watching. Waiting.

"I think you should hold still and listen for a bit, off-worlder," Kaljak said calmly. "Unless you don't particularly care for the lady. Then come ahead, by all means."

I took in the room in a glance and started running through options and trajectories.

"You can have her back, just get me those weapons," he continued. "I'm sure you have the list."

Before I could leap, a burly man chained to the table next to them lunged forward and threw the length of chain binding his wrist over Tyf's head, yanking him back.

"Myria, now!" I shouted, and she was already on the move, twisting away from Kaljak's grip.

She dropped down and rolled away, under the table, popping up on the far side.

Tyf's strangled gasps broke the silence as I barreled towards Kaljak, but he vaulted over the table, lips twisted in a snarl. With a jerk of his hand, he'd caught her, pulling her back by the scarf and twisting it tight around her neck.

"Not so fast, little bird," he sneered. "It's not time for you to fly away yet."

A thin woman rose from the table, her black hair badly chopped to frame her face. "Get your hands off my sister!" she screamed, and flung the bubbling contents of a beaker in Kaljak's face.

He screamed, hands clawing at the side of his face, and collapsed onto the floor.

Myria fell into the other woman's arms. "You're here, you're really here," she murmured. "I knew I'd find you."

The stranger stroked Myria's hair, tears streaming

down her face. "I can't believe you found me. But your poor neck..."

Myria looked up. "Aedan, this is my sister, Lira." Her eyes sparkled with mischief, and I knew that whatever trauma Kaljak had caused, my lady would be just fine. "You know, I've told you so much about her."

"Of course," I bowed. "If you'll allow me?" I snapped the chains binding Myria's sister, ripping out the hoop from the middle of the table.

The rest of the hall was in an uproar as the guards who had followed me fought with Kaljak's followers.

I needed every ally I could get. "I'll be right back," I promised Myria, then freed Narvin's son, stepping over the strangled body of Tyf at his feet. "Protect Myria, would you?" I asked.

"Of course. Dad would skin me alive if I didn't." He moved towards Myria and her sister, and I went to sort out the loyal guards from the soon-to-be-dead.

But even as I fought, I couldn't stop myself from checking, making sure she was still there, talking with her sister.

Healthy.

Laughing.

Mine.

MYRIA

"Good to see you again," Edrel grinned at me, then nodded shyly in Lira's direction.

I looked between them, mind whirling. "How do you two know each other?"

"We don't!" they blurted out together.

Lira looked away, cheeks on fire. "He was only brought in last night." Her eyes found his again before he turned away. "But since he's obviously a friend of yours, I'll take the recommendation."

But she kept sneaking looks at his broad back out of the corner of her eye, as he scanned the room, watching for signs of danger.

"I'd feel a lot more comfortable if we could move the two of you to a better protected location," he announced. "Not sure where that is, but this," he gestured to the melee sweeping up and down the room around us, "isn't it."

Lira set her jaw, then reached out and grabbed the hand of the woman chained next to her. "Move Myria somewhere else. I agree." Her knuckles went white. "But I have lived and worked with these people for too many years. I'm not abandoning them now. I won't leave until we're all free."

And that was my sister in a nutshell.

Not only beautiful and brilliant, but brave.

"I have so much to tell you." I leaned against her shoulder while we listened to the splintering of wood, the clash of swords, and the cries when someone was wounded.

She tugged a lock of hair that had escaped my braid. "You can start with telling me who your new friend is."

"I think he's more than a friend," I admitted. To her. To myself. Whatever was between us, we couldn't just let it stop, smothered to death in secrets and lies.

It took almost an hour for the chaos to subside, for Aedan to rally the loyal guards and free the prisoners.

"Safe enough?" I asked Edrel.

"I'll come with you," he said, but he looked torn at leaving Lira's side.

I kissed her cheek, then dashed around the wreckage to find Sweetie's mother. "I'm so sorry, I never asked your name."

"Rhyne," she blurted. "But where's my daughter?"

"Stay with me, and when we get out of here, I'll have someone take you to Sweetie right away." I caught myself. "Heidy," I corrected.

Rhyne wasn't shaking anymore, and her shoulders were back. "I'll be waiting, let's go."

In the chaos, the tables were smashed and the benches were overturned.

As Rhyne and I came back to where Lira waited, she watched it all. "In an odd way, Kaljak was right."

I stared at my sister, stunned.

"Oh, put down your eyebrows," she laughed. "I don't mean how he went about it, but what he was trying to do. Think of all the scientific advances that happened here."

She rubbed her wrists. "I would rather not have been chained for the entire time, but I have learned so much, we all have."

Edrel glanced over his shoulder and nodded once. "Even if the Empire were to come down tomorrow and give us the keys to spaceflight," he looked at me significantly, "we'd need to know how it all worked." His mouth twisted into a half-smile. "Otherwise it would be like handing a toy to a child and never explaining how it worked. Physics and chemistry, machines, those are our building blocks."

I squeezed my sister's hand. "You always did have a unique way of looking at things."

Soon enough, the room was quiet, a hush spreading as one by one, faces turned up to the viewing platform.

The elderly couple we'd found in the tower stood there, peering out over the room, flanked by Grohl and his fighters. The woman's face was marked by tears, but the man radiated fury.

"Wouldn't have thought so many were disloyal."

Aedan started to speak, but he cut him off. "Wasn't saying you were overzealous, boy, just mad at myself for letting things get out of control." He gave a short bow. "You've done me a favor by purging the traitors."

With a flick of his hand, Aedan sent an honor guard to accompany them as they descended the stairs and started to cross the wrecked room.

"I want to see the son of a bitch's body so I can spit on it," he said, then turned to the woman, and his voice gentled. "You may want to look away, my dear."

The woman rolled her eyes. "Jomu, if you think Imperial politics is less bloody than this room, you're going to be mightily surprised when we get to my nephew's coronation."

Wait, what?

That was Aedan's lost princess?

I'd half-wondered, but Kaljak had taken me from the tower before any explanations were made.

That wasn't the young, flighty girl I'd imagined. This was a grown woman, secure in her strength, even with her regalia stripped from her.

And Aedan thought he was going to drag her back somewhere she didn't want to be?

But as soon as I saw Grohl, all other thoughts left my mind.

"GROHL!" I shouted, hurrying towards him. "This is Sweetie's mother." The elderly couple looked confused, but honestly, they'd have to wait. "Can you take her back to the inn?"

"My dear lady, I knew this was all fated." He smiled, patted Rhyne's hand, and turned into the perfect host that brought travelers from across the region to his door.

"Let's get you back to the inn. I suspect there's a young lady who will be very excited to see you, no matter how many of Helene's cookies she's been eating."

Rhyne laughed in relief. "Sounds like she's been having quite an adventure."

I rubbed my forehead, suddenly worried about my temporary parenting abilities. "It's possible she's gotten a little attached to my torwynn, as well. Sorry about that."

"After this," Rhyne said, "all I want is to see her again. Everything else is negotiable." With Grohl chattering at her all the way, they went to retrieve her daughter.

Priorities.

Love. Family.

Everything else really should be negotiable, shouldn't it? I wondered.

"I'll miss that kid," Aedan said from behind me.

"Well, I'm glad one person is happy today," the old man growled. "Now I want to see someone who's about to have a very, very bad day."

But when we finished clearing away the wrecked tables, Kaljak was gone.

"I should've made sure he was dead," Aedan growled.

I twined my fingers around his, smoothing his hand until it unclenched. "Maybe there's been enough killing," I said.

He whirled on me, brilliant blue eyes like beacons. "He hurt you," he ground out. "He needs to pay."

"He hurt a lot of people," I said, and stepped closer to him. "I think we've had enough of living in the past."

In an instant, his arms were wrapped tightly around me and I breathed in the strange spicy scent of him.

"He could have killed you, and I never would've been able to say how sorry I was," he said into my hair.

I pulled back, just enough to see his face. “I'm sorry, too. I should've trusted you.”

He shook his head. “You're right, I’m not exactly the one to talk about having secrets. And that one, well, that wasn’t just yours to keep.” He brushed my hair back. “Still feel like being married?”

Lira popped up to the side of us. I’d forgotten how inconvenient having an older sister could be sometimes.

“Married? Really? Do tell me more. What exactly do you do for a living, Mr.… what was it?”

I buried my head in Aedan's shoulder, stifling laughter.

Edrel slowly approached Lira. “I suspect he comes with good references. I've only been here a day and I'm itching to stretch my legs.” He held a hand out towards my sister. “Would you like to go sit outside with me?”

For a moment, my sister's face tensed. “Outside,” she breathed. “It's been so long.”

My chest hurt, and I wiggled out of Aedan's embrace. “Come on,” I said, guilt lashing at me. “I should go with you. We have lots to catch up on.”

“Oh no,” she said, and shoved me back towards Aedan. “It sounds like you have business of your own to handle. We can catch up later.” She shot Aedan a stern look. “But if you hurt her…” she trailed off.

Aedan held his hands up. “I’ve already seen what

you can do. I don't plan on giving you any cause for worry."

"Hmnph," Lira answered, then wandered off, talking softly with Edrel.

"Do you think she's really alright?" I asked Aedan as I watched her leave the room.

"If she's been a prisoner here for all that time, she's going to need a period of adjustment, the ability to do things at her own pace," he answered, wrapping an arm around me. "But if she's anywhere as strong as you are, she'll be fine. We'll just give her time."

"*We'll* give her time?" I looked up at him, curious about his choice of pronoun.

He took advantage of my upturned face to kiss me, long and deep, until I melted against him. "You never did answer me, you know."

"Jomu, don't you think the children should have a break?" a warm, rich voice interrupted whatever I was going to say.

I pulled back, to find the princess and Flame watching us with absolutely no shame, her hand idly playing with her necklace.

Cheeks burning, I pulled the scarf from around my neck, folded it carefully, and held it out. "I think this belongs to you, your Highness."

She took it and ran it through her hands. "I wonder how it made its way to you," she murmured, then stepped forward to drape it back around my neck. "It's much prettier on you. And do call me Ellie, won't you?"

If there'd been any doubts that Ellie was a princess, they were quickly resolved when she took the re-ordering of the castle in hand.

Before I knew what happened, Aedan and I had been whisked away into a luxurious room, with a tall four-poster bed with a thick mattress and comfortable looking pillows against one wall and plush rugs across the floor, all in a deep green.

I thought it was lovely, but she clucked at the state of the wall hangings and the dryness of the wood.

"I do wonder what that man has been doing for housekeepers for the last sixty years," she tutted. "I would have it aired out fresh, but I think you're not really going to be paying attention, are you, my dears?" She patted Aedan's cheek and he blinked.

"Do try to eat something at some point," she added, motioning for a bewildered looking guard to set a plate of fruits and cheeses on top of a low chest. "I suspect you both need to keep your energy up."

And in a whirl of skirts, she swept out the door.

"Are all the women in the Empire like that?" I wondered aloud, more than a little stunned.

"Maybe not quite like that, but I've learned to just let them do what they want," Aedan answered. "It's safer that way."

A pitcher of steaming hot water and fresh towels were brought to the room next.

I eyed the tray of fruit longingly, but after an entire day spent searching the air shafts, being kidnapped, and fighting, I was filthy. "If I don't get cleaned up first, I'll just spoil all of it."

"I could help you wash," Aedan offered. "Then you can have dinner twice as fast."

"I don't think so," I grabbed a towel, dipped a corner into the hot water, and started scrubbing at my hands and face. "Neither of us will get clean that way."

He grinned. "You know me too well."

I sat down on the bed suddenly, knees weak and gut hollow with more than hunger. "But isn't that the issue? What I know, what I don't?"

He froze. "I think," he said slowly, "you know me in every way that matters."

He took a deep breath, eyes searching my face. "Except for one thing. Those horrors, the monsters the warlords created like that thing in the river. I'm not that different."

"I know," I whispered, "I'm sorry."

His eyes widened a fraction. "So it does matter to you," he said.

"What? No!" I exclaimed, shooting to my feet. "I'm sorry that I didn't understand sooner." I went to hold his hands, to tangle my fingers with his. To hell with the dust and the grime and the blood. It would all wash away, but if we didn't get this straight, we'd never be really free from this day.

"I don't care what you are, how you were made, where you came from," I insisted. "I know you." I looked up, and risked a smile as I met those startling sapphire eyes. "But I wouldn't mind getting to know you better," I continued, "and for that, you just need to tell me the truth, not assume that I won't accept it."

Standing on my toes, I stretched up to press a kiss on his lips. "I love you, no matter what."

Slowly, reverently, he drew the clothing off me, and this time I didn't stop him.

I pulled the clothes off his hard body, letting my fingers roam over his chest, and when we were clean, we tumbled into the bed.

Dropping kisses down my neck, his lips and hands lightly roamed over my skin, turning me to kindling, burning me, pushing me to the edge with every touch.

Until, at an involuntary hiss when he brushed the edge of the bandage at my neck, he stopped. "You've had a long day," he insisted, rolling away from me, "And we haven't had dinner yet, and-"

Reaching down, I stroked the hard length of his cock. "I'm not hungry for dinner anymore," I purred as he groaned, eyes closing. "I have other things on my mind." I ran my fingers back down and up again, watching the straining muscle in his jaw.

Then I leaned to lick the muscle. "Stop treating me like glass," I whispered, then nipped at his collarbone. "Husband."

His eyes flew open, and before the word had fully left my lips, we'd rolled, him pinning me beneath him, then propping up on his elbows to look down at me.

"You're sure?" he asked, voice threaded with a vulnerability I'd never heard before.

"I'm sure," I looked into those eyes and saw all the stars I'd ever want, all the future I'd ever need. I slid my arms up to wrap around his back, pulling him down towards me. "Wherever it leads, I'm sure of that."

"But right now?" I ran my nails down his back, felt him grow unbelievably harder against me. "I'm sure of other things, too."

And then, whatever control he had broke.

AEDAN

I ground my hips against her, not entering those silken folds, not yet, just needing to feel her squirm beneath me, hear her breathing change, to watch as her pupils dilated, her gaze grew wild.

"You'd better be sure," I growled as I licked my way down her throat, into the valley between her breasts, stopping to tease one and then the other, licking and nipping at the tight buds until she cried out.

"Because I don't think I can let you go," I kept working down her belly, kneeling between her thighs as I lifted her towards me.

"Not now," I licked the crease of her leg, stopping before reaching her mound, digging my fingers into the curve of her hips as she moaned, the maddening scent of her arousal perfuming the air.

"Not ever." And then I couldn't hold off any longer. I fell on her, licking and sucking and devouring, her cries of release only spurring me on, driving me to take her to new heights as she spasmed again and again.

Her fingers knotted in my hair as I slid one finger in to work her tight core while I sucked at her clit, and then another, until with a final shout, she sprawled, loose and relaxed.

"My Myria," I groaned as I crawled back over her, watching her eyes flutter open.

"My wife," I breathed as my throbbing cock barely brushed against her slick folds.

She smiled and tilted her hips up, drawing me closer. "Mate," I whispered, as slowly, so slowly, I drove inside her, so that by the time I was fully sheathed in her heat, we were both trembling.

"I love you." My eyes locked with hers. "Forever."

And I was finally home.

THE MORNING LIGHT had barely touched the deep green rugs when I woke to a familiar rumble.

Landing jets.

It was time.

"Myria," I said softly, brushing her sleep-tangled

hair back from her face. "We're about to have company."

"Hmm?" she whimpered softly. "Too early, tell them to come back later."

Mornings were never going to be her favorite time of day, I could tell.

I had already begun to pull on my pants when the pounding on the door started.

"Sir!" someone shouted. "There's a spaceship. In the courtyard."

"Yes," I called through the door, glancing at the lump under the covers where Myria had burrowed back down. She'd have to wake up anyway, I supposed. "I invited them."

"Oh," his voice faltered. "Flame, Jomu, he…"

I took pity on the messenger standing and yelling in the hallway and opened the door a crack.

"You mean the real one, the old guy, right?"

He nodded, and I sympathized. It had been a confusing day for everyone.

"He asked if you'd come down to the courtyard and deal with it," he swallowed. "The spaceship, I mean. Please."

"I doubt if he said anything quite so nicely, but I'll be there in a minute." I closed the door and for a moment, spaceships and princesses all fell away as I took in the glorious sight of Myria sitting up, blinking, sheets crumpled at her waist.

"Did he say spaceship?"

I nodded. "Just outside. Come on, let's go see who's here."

Faster than I'd ever seen her move, she'd slid back into her clothes, grabbed her scarf, and was braiding her hair as we walked down the hall.

"There were rumors that a spaceship came down here once before," she mumbled around her hair tie. "This will set all the gossips on fire."

"I think," I said as I gave her a hand down the stone stairs, watching her feet since she certainly wasn't, "that ship must have been Eladia's personal craft, bringing her here. It's impressive. Even if she's been waiting all this time for her brother's surveillance to slip, he must have wielded considerable influence with her guards."

Myria rolled her eyes at me. "Or affection, you know." She tied off her braid and threw it back over her shoulder. "Either way, I can't imagine anyone getting in the way of what she wants."

"Let's go see how she handles it." I wrapped my hand around hers. "Kinda looking forward to watching the show."

The gleaming silver ship towered over the courtyard, blackened stones below it still scorching with the transferred heat from atmospheric entry.

Myria gasped at the destruction, and I wrapped an

arm around her shoulders. "It would have been worse if we hadn't found her," I reminded her. "Much worse."

The hatch slid open and pairs of guards in short flowing crimson capes marched down, spreading into a menacing circle.

"You can knock it off," I hollered up the ramp, assuming Vandalar was monitoring everything. "The situation isn't what you think."

The guards didn't blink. Vandalar must have warned them about reacting. Shame, took away half the fun.

But Vandalar himself came down the ramp quickly enough, dressed practically for a change. Maybe his impending responsibilities had impressed on him the value of a more restrained demeanor.

"Alright, then where is she?" he demanded.

Or not.

"Probably making you wait," I answered. "She came here of her own accord, and isn't super thrilled about being forced to return."

"What?"

"There's a lot you don't know, but I expect she'll tell you on the way back." I grinned as his eyes narrowed. "Also, I hope you have room for an extra passenger. She's bringing a guest to the festivities."

He raised an elegant eyebrow. "While you might be comfortable bouncing around the galaxy in tiny, ramshackle crafts, I assure you my great-aunt has different standards."

Oh, this was going to be good.

And the fireworks would start just as soon as Eladia got here.

I started to worry, then pushed it to the side. She was an old lady, probably took longer to get ready in the mornings. She probably wanted to punish her nephew a little bit. It wouldn't hurt him to wait.

Vandalar turned to Myria, flashing his smarmy smile. "And this is?"

I growled. "None of your business."

"Seriously?" Myria kicked my ankle. "He's your sister's friend. Be polite."

Vandalar smothered a laugh. "I suspect Loree will be able to tell me all about her soon enough." Then the casual look fell away as the sound of running boots pounding on stone approached. "That doesn't sound like my great-aunt either."

It wasn't.

Jomu burst into the courtyard, leaning heavily on his cane, surrounded by a quartet of guards, all in the signature orange and black. "Is she with you?"

Oh, Void.

"Isn't that interesting?" Vandalar said icily, his face grim. "One might almost think that those colors indicate a certain nom de guerre, a certain someone I'd be very interested in speaking with."

With a snap, his guards faced off with Jomu's, matching stance with stance. Except Vandalar's men carried blasters. Swords would have no chance.

"Stop it," Myria grabbed Vandalar's arm and shook it. He looked down on her, remote mask in place. "You don't know what's going on here, and if you keep that up, you never will."

"I believe I require an explanation, then, quickly," he demanded.

"None of this is quick, or easy," I said. "The whole thing is a tangle, and your grandfather's fault in more ways than one." I pointed to Jomu. "See him? That guy is quite literally an old flame of Eladia's.

"She came to Kerrind to visit him, figuring no one would notice she was missing in all the hubbub at the capital." I shrugged, hoping Vandalar would see it like she had. "The old emperor's sister, the aging great-aunt of the new guy. She didn't think it would be a big deal."

"Except that's not what happened," he cut in.

"Actually, that's exactly what happened. But while she was here, someone impersonated Flame's dataprint and sent off that list of demands. A usurper, who took advantage of the situation."

Alright. Maybe that wasn't exactly what had happened, but it was close.

"Her old boyfriend didn't know anything about the ransom. They were pretty happily, um, well, playing house when we got here."

Vandalar swallowed hard. "I don't need that level of detail. If that's the case, where is she?"

"It's been a busy couple of days," I tried to explain. "We got rid of the usurper, freed a bunch of enslaved budding scientists, discovered secret passages, and made a general mess of the castle. And your great-aunt? She's a bundle of energy. She could be anywhere, organizing anything."

"And that's the important part for you to know," Myria said. "Ellie really could be anywhere, doing anything, because she wants to." She stepped forward, back rigid. "She likes it here, likes being useful, and loves being with that man." She pointed to Jomu, who colored, but didn't say anything. "Her brother separated them all those years ago. Why should you be the one that tells her where to go, who to love?"

I fought to keep my face neutral. For a brief moment, I'd worried that Myria might be overawed by the Imperial Splendor.

Apparently not.

"I'm not trying to tell her where she can or can't go," Vandalar said, tugging at his hair in frustration. "I'm trying to make sure she's safe. If she'd just told me where she was going...." he trailed off, and an edge of fear cut through me.

"I mentioned that to her when I found her," I said aloud, slowly. "She wouldn't run again, not knowing the consequences." I waved at the damn guards. "Tell your men to stand down, we have a problem."

"That's why they're on alert," muttered Vandalar, but he gave the order.

"Jomu, call them off!" I shouted across the courtyard, and in moments the old man was with us.

"She's not in the castle," he said, with barely a glance at Vandalar.

"And she didn't leave a note, anything?" The thought worried at me, wouldn't leave me alone.

"I've been up most of the night, clearing out the mess you made," Jomu answered. "Don't worry about it, should never have let things get that far out of hand. More my fault than yours."

"I assume someone will fill me in on the details shortly?" Vandalar asked mildly.

"Once I'm sure you're less of a torwynn's ass than your grandfather, I'll consider it," Jomu snapped. "And until Ellie's safe, I don't have time for extraneous people."

Before Vandalar could respond, Myria stepped in. "We're all worried, and snapping at each other isn't going to help. When's the last time anyone saw her?"

Jomu rubbed his forehead. “One of the staff thinks she saw her early this morning, helping an injured man. But that was hours ago.”

The worry bloomed into an icy fear. “Injured? How?”

“Bandages all around his head, she said,” Jomu answered, then paled. “You don’t think…?”

“It must be,” I said flatly. “I should have hunted the bastard down immediately.”

“But why would she go with him?” Myria wondered.

“She never met him, never knew him as anything other than one of my captains,” Jomu said angrily. “If he’d said he was injured, she'd have helped him.”

“Or if he told her you’d been injured,” Myria said, hand clutching at her scarf. “She wouldn’t leave a note, because she thought she was on her way to you.”

There was no time to wonder or worry, to regret what had or hadn’t been done.

“We’ll widen the search,” Jomu announced. “Track anyone who-”

“Hurry!” came a shout from the far side of the courtyard, as Rhyne ran around the corner, breathless and pale.

Myria ran forward to grab the woman’s thin arms. “What’s happened?”

“That man came back to the tavern,” Rhyne gasped

for breath, voice shaking. “He grabbed Heidy when she went out to feed your torwynn.”

“What? Who?” Myria asked, but I already knew the answer.

“Kaljak.”

MYRIA

Jomu's guards cleared the way for us as we dashed back to the town, and Grohl met us as we turned into the neighborhood of the tavern.

"She just wanted to go see Dayla," he sputtered, face as gray as his hair as he ran with us. "Padsu came back without her, scared and cut." I'd never seen him so rattled, not when we were conspiring against Flame, not in the tunnels.

This was different.

"Padsu said a man was waiting in the stables, grabbed Sweetie away, and said he'd snap her neck if he didn't get what he wanted, to get the bard and the soldier."

Rhyne whimpered.

"Not happening," Aedan growled, and we ran faster.

We burst into the inn to find Helene holding the boy, dabbing at a long cut across a cheekbone.

"I tried to fight him, I did!" Padsu cried, chin trembling. "But he had a knife, and…"

"You did your best," Aedan said gruffly, "then you went for reinforcements, and brought back valuable information. That's all you could've done."

"What if he hurts Dayla, too?" he sniffled.

"Dayla can look after herself," I said, hoping it was true, knowing that words didn't really matter now. "But you're thinking of the torwynn and the human, both. You'll make a fine trainer."

Rhyne stepped forward and hugged the boy. "You were very brave. She's got a good friend in you."

"Sweetie's tougher than you realize," I said, resting a hand on his head. "I'll bet you she hasn't even told you about leaping across that chasm while riding Dayla. Didn't blink an eye."

Neither Rhyne or Padsu looked comforted.

"We'll get her back," I echoed.

"Whatever it takes," Aedan growled.

"I've got snipers stationed around the building," Vandalar said, tapped a black button in his ear. "As soon as they have a clear stream, they'll take it."

"Snipers?" Rhyne gasped. "Streams? Do you mean lasers?" If possible, she paled even further. "Around Heidy? Who are you?"

This time, I kicked Vandalar's ankle instead of Aedan's. "He's a friend, and he's trying to help."

I backed away from the front room and headed towards the courtyard with Aedan, Jomu, and Vandalar.

"Is there any other way into the stables?" Aedan asked. "Any more of those tunnels?"

Grohl shook his head. "You could try going in the side where we load the branches for the zugrin, but the gate squeaks. Been meaning to get it fixed for years." He eyed Jomu warily. "Had other things on my mind."

Aedan and Jomu looked ready for a fight, but Rhyne was right. We couldn't risk it, not if Kaljak had Sweetie.

But, if she was his hostage, where was Ellie?

"If she thought a child was at risk, Ellie would have gone with him, no questions," Jomu mused. "Might have been how he got her out of the castle."

"Spy drones would be useful about now," Aedan commented. "Don't suppose you brought any with you?"

Vandalar threw up his hands. "Somehow I didn't think to bring any with me. First, they're not part of my regular packing list. Second, because someone sent the message that he'd already acquired my aunt."

"Her name is Eladia, boy, and she's not something to be acquired," Jomu snarled.

"That's it," I decided. "I'm going to see what's going on. We don't even know for certain that it's Kaljak."

"The hell you are," Aedan snarled.

I put a hand on his arm. "I'm not saying I'm letting him near me, but of the four of us, I'm the one he's less likely to feel threatened by."

"Only because he's never been kicked by you," Vandalar muttered, and I ignored him.

"Also," I narrowed my eyes at Aedan, "you don't get to tell me what to do, husband."

He pulled me into a tight embrace. "I've just found you. You can't blame me for not wanting to lose you."

"You won't," I promised. "I'm trusting you to get all of us out alive. And you know I'm the best opening move we've got."

"She's right," Jomu admitted. "But if he's hurt Ellie..." he trailed off and for a moment the tyrant of old shone through clearly the old man's eyes.

"Let's get this started," I said as I pushed away from Aedan's comforting arms. "You can argue over who gets to kill him after everyone is safe."

Rounding the corner of the inn, I strode towards the long, low building that housed the stables. Zugrin lumbered at the far right, stomping and swaying as they pulled at their breakfast from the rack.

"Stop!" came a shout from a familiar voice. "Walk slower. I want to see you clearly."

Kaljak, no question.

"It wasn't that long ago you said that I kept running

to you," I called back to the deep shadows, the clean smell of norvell branches perfuming the air, proclaiming this was just another normal morning, even though there was nothing normal about it at all.

"Little bird, have you come to give yourself up, as well?" he called back. "Decided to join me after all?"

"No," I said firmly. "I'm just here to find out what you want. You hurt the boy, you know. If you wanted him to carry a message, you'd have done better not to frighten him."

He laughed, the sound shrill and mocking. "I think it worked out well enough. You're here, aren't you?"

"I want to see Sweetie, make sure she's unharmed, before we talk any further."

Kaljak stepped out of the shadows, his orange and black coat ripped and tattered. Bandages covered one side of his face, his eye peering and milky. But I only cared about the silent, wide-eyed child on his hip. "So what are you going to do, little bird? Negotiate for the little girl or the old hag?"

That answered one question, unless Kaljak was being clever. And he was, really. Mad, but clever.

"Ellie, are you there? Are you alright?" I called.

"She'll stay back if she knows what's good for the brat," Kaljak snapped.

Claws of ice gripped my stomach, but years of

training helped keep my voice even. “If you have her, I need to know.”

Kaljak sighed dramatically. “Fine,” he called over his shoulder. “You can answer.”

“I'm here,” Ellie said from the shadows. “I’m fine.”

Kaljak pinched Sweetie’s arm savagely, and she yelped.

“What did you do that for?” I cried out. “You told her she could answer!”

“The old lady knows that’s the price of making a sound. The brat will pay it.”

“WHAT DO YOU WANT?” I called out. “You can’t plan to stay in that stable forever.”

Out of the corner of my eye, I thought I saw movement, a quickness out of place so close to the plodding zugrin.

Aedan. And whatever he was doing, he’d need time.

One step closer to the stables. Another.

“I know you always want something,” I smoothed my voice, sent it out as a lure. “You have all the cards now.”

“Go get the ambassador,” he barked. “Now that he’s here, I want to trade for weapons.”

Ambassador? I blinked, confused, and Sweetie shrieked again.

"Don't try to stall, bitch," he snarled. "Everyone in town saw the ship land this morning."

Right.

"Ambassador Vand?" I called over my shoulder, hoping that the heir to the Empire was as clever as the man holed up in a stable, would pick up on the stress of his new title and name. "He'd like to talk with you."

"Coming!" he sang out, and I nearly choked as His Royal Highness Vandalar, crown prince to the Empire, Emperor in all but name, sashayed into the courtyard.

"This really is most irregular," he scolded me. "I was told that negotiations were to happen at that drafty castle. Horrid enough, and now to be rushed here! You've been unforgivably rude."

Arm thrown in the air, he advanced towards the stables. "I assume you're the one who sent the higher ups that shopping list? We've started unloading it, back there. We'll have to move it all over again, of course, unless the castle is your permanent place of residence?"

Kaljak stepped back, and Vandalar stopped, waiting. Watching.

Buying more time for Aedan, I realized.

"Did you not want the weapons, after all?" He waved towards Sweetie dismissively. "The local woman might care about the child, but I don't. I need to see the Princess Eladia before we continue our little chat."

"Old woman," Kaljak snapped. "There's someone here to see you."

Silently, Ellie emerged from the shadows, dress crumpled, hair still braided tightly back. A darkening bruise discolored one cheekbone, but she held her chin high with defiance.

Vandalar's eyes flashed dangerously, but his tone stayed light, petty. "Your Highness, when you're safely onboard, I'll instruct your guards to deliver the weapons to this brigand."

"Ambassador, I'm not going anywhere until that child is safely in the arms of her mother," Ellie's voice rang out.

"That's a shame," Kaljak said. "Because I'm not letting her go. She's my insurance for your behavior. If I don't have her, and I don't have you, I'm not going to get my weapons."

I stepped forward, chest tight. "But you'll have me."

Ellie gasped, and I thought I heard Vandalar swear under his breath.

But Kaljak just tilted his head to the side, thinking.

"You said earlier that you wanted me, and the weapons, but you couldn't have both." I took another step forward, and then another. "What if you can now?"

I didn't need to hear Aedan's disapproval. I could feel it in the air, in my head. But he'd have to understand, agree.

Sweetie had to come first.

"You'd come with me, willingly?" Kaljak mused. "In exchange for what?"

"You have to let the girl go." I nodded towards Sweetie. "You'd have me to ensure the princess's cooperation." Another step closer. "And then they have to give you the weapons, to get her back."

Vandalar sniffed loudly. "I can only repeat this is a very, very irregular proceeding. I'll be making a report to my superiors as soon as we've returned."

Kaljak's eyes flicked back and forth between us, caught up in the decision. The possibilities.

And then a dark form rose from behind Kaljak, darker than the surrounding shadows.

Aedan, I almost breathed aloud. Finally.

But the shadow kept rising, growing taller and more distinct until with a gasp, I could make out the shape.

"No!" Kaljak screamed, as Dayla's talons raked down his spine, jerking him backwards.

Sweetie fell from his arms and Aedan swooped down from the rafters, catching her before she hit the ground and rolling away with her.

Jomu charged in to pull Ellie to safety, but there was no threat.

Not any longer.

Dayla had used her short arms to the best of their abilities, slashing and yanking at Kaljak until he'd fallen back, and now she calmly trampled him while stretching up for more norvell leaves.

"Pretty Dayla," Sweetie mumbled against Aedan's shoulder, while Kaljak's screams brought Grohl and Rhyne to the courtyard.

"Let's go inside," I said quickly, herding them back, knowing the others would follow. "Everything's alright now. It's over."

EXCEPT OF COURSE, there were complications.

Rhyne and Helene examined Heidy, but red pinch marks were the only visible signs of her ordeal.

Vandalar and Jomu sent their guards to clean up the stables. Padsu wanted to go with them to move Dayla, but Grohl insisted that part of his torwynn training would have to wait for a few years.

Jomu accompanied them. "Want to make sure the...scoundrel is really done for," he explained. "If you don't need me around for a few minutes?" he asked Ellie.

She patted his cheek. "I've told you twelve times already, I'm fine. Annoyed to be taken in so easily by that man's trick, that's all." She turned to Vandalar with narrowed eyes. "And that gives me some time to talk with my dear nephew."

"I still don't understand what you're doing here," Vandalar complained. "How did you even know this place existed?"

Her lips pursed. "And here I was hoping you'd be cleverer than my brother. Apparently we're all due for a sad disappointment."

Jomu returned from the stable, and she slipped her arm in the crook of his elbow. "All those years ago, Kerrind was torn apart by civil war. Risking everything, one of their leaders made his way back to the Hub in a rickety old spaceship, begging for help for his world."

"It wasn't that old," Jomu muttered. "Got me there, didn't it?"

"As you know, my brother refused," Eladia continued. "What you don't know is that we fell in love. And my brother refused to acknowledge that, as well."

"But," Vandalar sputtered, "that was years ago!"

I looked at Eladia. "I think it's your turn to kick him."

"Very likely," she smiled serenely, "but I'll wait until he's not expecting it."

Vandalar pulled at his hair. "You can kick me all you like, as long as we're on the way back to the Hub."

My heart cracked, just a bit. No matter what promises we'd made in the bedroom, in the heat of danger and passion, I knew the truth. Everything was over, and Aedan would be gone.

"How long do we have before the coronation?" Eladia asked. "Jomu and I have some catching up to do, and neither of us plan to be cooped up in the capital."

She held up a hand to stop Vandalar as he opened his mouth to speak. "We will be there for the ceremony, I promise." Her eyes narrowed. "I will even be polite to my brother. Don't ask for more."

Vandalar nodded. "That's fair enough." He stood, and the guards lining the walls snapped to attention. "There's plenty of room shipboard for your guest."

Standing straighter, I focused on my breathing, on calming my pounding heart. It's no different than facing an ugly crowd, I told myself. I've done it before, I can do-

"I'm not going back with you," Aedan announced.

Vandalar blinked. "The mission is over, but if you think there's a need to stay, keep an eye on things…"

"Nope. Just like it here. Figured I'd stay for a bit."

Aedan turned me gently until I faced him. "You didn't think I'd make you leave with me, did you? Choose between seeing your sister and going with me?"

I shook my head numbly. "But your brothers, your whole life is out there."

His lips on mine were more of a promise than a kiss. "My whole life is right here, right before me. Wherever you are." He scowled, just a bit. "But I'd be less eager to

tell you where you should go if I knew you weren't likely to make stupid offers to maniacs."

"Doc will have my head if I don't bring you back," Vandalar rambled behind me, but I didn't care, couldn't hear anything but the words of the man who held me. "That AI of yours will sabotage every ship in my fleet."

"You'd really stay here, give all of it up," I asked, searching his face, trying to find the truth. "The stars, all those worlds, everything?"

"I have a whole world here," he said, and held me tighter, then I melted for a moment against his hard strength before pushing back.

"What if I want to see it?" I asked. "Even just once?"

"If that's what you want, then we'll go. Nothing says we can't go out to the stars and come back, not anymore." He glanced at Jomu. "I'm assuming the technology ban is lifted?"

"What? Oh, I suppose."

Ellie raised one eyebrow at him, and he shrugged. "Wasn't going to last for much longer anyway."

"How convenient." She leaned into his shoulder, smiling. "Nephew, I think a small ship would make an excellent wedding present."

And they might have said something more, but I was lost in Aedan's kiss, our future bright before us, no more shadows, no more lies.

Limitless.

AEDAN

"So you're really going back?" Davien asked as we watched the women around the Zoombies table. Over the last week, Loree and Nadira had taken turns teaching everyone the rules of the game, and now Myria cackled with glee as she set her holographic army against Zadya's.

"They need the help," I said, taking a long drink of my brew. "And Myria's just found her sister again."

"Seems like she's not short on sisters now," he said, pointing to the games table where the battle had broken up. "Kara was saying she might want to visit, have a chance to get a little dirty. She said it sounded like fun."

His lip curled into a snarl. "You would have thought she'd gotten enough of that fighting for her life against Xavis."

"Actually..." I trailed off.

Heart-to-heart talks weren't a thing any of us were good at. I'd rather go one-on-one against another Hunter.

If we'd left any of them alive.

But there was no backing out now. Davien waited, one eyebrow arched.

"Maybe you should talk to Kara about that whole staying safe thing. Seems like with her particular skill set, it might be better for her to find something interesting to do, rather than get bored."

"Really? What makes you such an expert?" he asked coldly.

"Because I would have given anything to keep Myria safe. And she's stronger than that." I punched his arm, just friendly like. Brotherly. "Besides, Kara would kick my ass if I told you any more. So just talk to her, would you?"

Whatever Davien was about to say was drowned out when all the speakers in the dive muted, started playing a soft chiming melody.

The lights dimmed, and in a swirl of golden light, the hologram above the Zoombies table reshaped itself, the battleground transforming to a three-quarters image of a girl in her late teens.

"Who the hell is that?" I snapped, heart pounding,

ready to go, prepared for whatever the next emergency was. "And how did they hack our systems?"

"No idea," Davien answered.

Two high ponytails of blue and purple strands cascaded from the top of her head, the shimmering skin tone shifting as the image rotated, scanning the room with solid black eyes.

There you are! she exclaimed, and we all winced.

"Nixie?" Kara gasped.

Doc said I should find you quickly! It's time!

She blinked out of existence, and the lights and sounds of the bar returned to normal.

Myria grabbed my hand, and I stumbled behind her, mind still catching up.

It was time.

Eris and Connor's baby was coming.

And somehow, Nixie had generated a body.

Whatever else the universe could throw at us, one thing was for certain.

Family was strange.

And worth everything.

After she'd had a nap and a bath, Eris had insisted on her bed being moved to a corner of the main room of the small house she and Connor had claimed as their own.

"Not interested in being away from the action," she'd announced. And with Doc and Nadira on either side of her, Connor had reluctantly agreed.

Loree held the newborn girl carefully so that Vicki could see the tiny red face. "That's not really how babies are supposed to look, is it?" She'd pulled back, brow wrinkled. "Why didn't you just keep her in a tube until she was all the way ready?"

Val pulled her into a hug. "Because in this family, people come in all sorts of ways. And they're still family, got it?"

"I guess..." Vicki said, but she didn't look convinced.

Midair, Nixie's new holographic form beamed at her younger sister, and Granny Z waited impatiently for another turn to hold the baby and sing slightly sinister lullabies.

Wolves and their mates crammed into the room, all of us eager to see the newest member of the pack. Another mark of our survival, a victory against the odds.

"I'm glad we were here for this," Myria said, leaning back against me. "This is special."

"Doesn't scare you off?" I answered, wrapping my arms around her waist. "I know it's probably a little much." Bending over her neck, I breathed in the sweet smell of her. "Hell, they're all a little much for me sometimes."

"Good thing we've got a planet to get back to, then," she said, sarcasm dripping. "Because everything there is so neat and orderly. You volunteered for one hell of a job."

"Thanks for reminding me," I groaned. Vandalar had tried to appoint me Imperial Governor of Kerrind. That lasted for a minute, while I had Loree punch in Helene's data and send it back.

Helene and her father knew the world, knew the people. A network of tavern owners and bards would provide all the information we could possibly need. Lira and Edrel had agreed to start a new technology and education department, slowly rolling out the new advances while teaching the world how to use them.

And I'd be there to help negotiate the transition, especially during Jomu and Eladia's long-delayed honeymoon.

Myria turned in my arms, eyes laughing. "And despite everything, you love it."

"No, I love you." I kissed her, tasting forever on her lips. "As long as you can put up with me being an occasional idiot."

"I think I can manage that," she promised.

And she did.

. . .

THE END

COMING UP NEXT?

Quinn is off to investigate a mysterious signal…

HE WAS THERE to find his brothers. Not his mate.

Quinn is hot on the trail of a missing squadron of the Star Breed. Navigating the politics of the mega-corps that run this sector doesn't leave him time for much else.

Certainly no time for smart, passionate Trini.

But when Trini turns out to be the key to finding a lost brother, can he keep to his mission, and keep her safe?

CLICK HERE to get Crossed now!

BE sure you've either signed up for my newsletter, joined the facebook group, or both!

And please don't forget to leave a review. I love reading what you think of the books!

. . .

XOXO,

Elin

P.S. KEEP READING for the first bit of Vrehx, book one of my alien romance series, Conquered World!

PLEASE DON'T FORGET TO LEAVE A REVIEW!

Readers rely on your opinions, and your review can help others decide on what books they read. Make sure your opinion is heard and leave a review where you purchased this book!

Don't miss a new release! You can sign up for release alerts at both Amazon and Bookbub:

bookbub.com/authors/elin-wyn

amazon.com/author/elinwyn

For a free short story, opportunities for advance review copies, release news and the occasional cat picture, please join the newsletter!

https://elinwynbooks.com/newsletter-signup/

And don't forget the Facebook group, where I post sneak peeks of chapters and covers!

https://www.facebook.com/groups/ElinWyn/

DON'T MISS THE CONQUERED WORLD!

He shattered her world. Can she trust him with her heart?

Giant spiders, walking trees, bloodthirsty vines.

For Jeneva, it's just another day trying to survive in the jungles of Ankau.

Until the sky ripped open, and the true monsters came through.

Now her world is under attack, and the only place of safety may be at the side of a rock-hard scaled alien.

But he's filled with secrets - how can she trust him?

Vrehx cares for nothing other than the destruction of the Xathi hordes who burned his home and killed his family.

But when a weapons test goes horribly wrong, the battle spills over to an uncharted world.

The planet is filled with lethal native life...but nothing is more dangerous than the human woman who obsesses his thoughts.

When war rages around them, can they fight together, or will his burning need for her drive them apart?

Vrehx is the first book in the science fiction romance series Conquered World. Each book is a new romance with alpha male alien warriors and women who don't put up with their nonsense. No cheating, no cliffhangers, HEA guaranteed!

Click to get Vrehx now or keep reading for a sample!

https://elinwynbooks.com/conquered-world-alien-romance/

VREHX

Streaks of plasma lit the blackness as a squadron of Valorni fighters swooped in dizzying spirals, blasting at the massive Xathi ship that filled the screens of the *Vengeance*.

We were so close it was the size of a planet. Like two steel ziggurats smashed and welded together. Not practical for space flight, but efficient enough to tear through several worlds.

Designed to intimidate.

Designed to destroy.

And we were going to stop it.

We crept closer, waiting. I sucked in my breath, geared for the inevitable.

I gritted my teeth as the bridge shook, and Karzin let out an undignified whoop from his station on the far curve of the bridge. The purple stripes on his shoulders rippled, and his excited eyes darted back and forth as if cheering on his favorite sport.

Barbarian. His crude Valorni traits got on my last nerve—not that he gave a rat's ass. Like the lot of them, he had no empathy for others. He barely listened to commands and forget anyone who didn't at least match his rank.

"You green motherfuckers aren't supposed to be hitting us, just laying cover for our approach," I snarled. "They can remember that much, can't they?"

They had only begun venturing into space when we took them into the alliance, but surely they weren't that stupid.

I hoped not.

"Fuck you," the Valorni drawled. The stretched-out

sounds of his abominable accent were like bristles to my red Skotan scales. "Not their fault we're cloaked all to hell."

What an asshole. Valorni couldn't even be bothered to speak accurately. Their drawl made it nearly impossible to understand them, and they had idiotic slang for everything.

"They were informed of our flight path before the battle." The lights of Sk'lar's implants flickered in the dim light of the bridge. "It should have been simple for them to avoid it."

I smiled just a little, glad I wasn't the only one with some common sense. Sk'lar wasn't much better than Karzin, but he was more tolerable. My biggest problem was his implants.

His artificial augmentation was just creepy and wrong. You could see them light up in biohazard green against his shiny black skin. He looked like a fucking motherboard.

The strike team leaders were chosen for their specific talents and leadership, but Sk'lar's was not stealth outside the ship.

Karzin made it a point to butt heads with all of us. That usually distracted the rest of us from being at each other's throats.

Maybe that was his intention. Whatever. He was an asshole.

Karzin shrugged off the K'ver's barely concealed criticism. "Not gonna matter in a few minutes, is it?"

The sarcasm warranted him a disapproving side-eye from Sk'lar, which he ignored. I hated to admit it, but the jackass was right. In a few minutes, we would probably all be dead.

"Gentlemen," Rouhr's quiet word from the command station silenced the chatter, "are you prepared?"

The scar that ran down the left side of his face rippled as he clenched his jaw. He was annoyed.

Of course, we were prepared.

We shut up anyway. Rouhr was very diplomatic. That's why he was in charge.

We straightened ourselves and regained our concentration.

Tension and anger clogged the air, but there was no fear. Fear had died when our families did, when our worlds had burned under the Xathi attacks.

Around the half circle, each of us activated the new weapons panels, the long seconds drawing out as they lit up and hummed. Every battle had this moment—the waiting before the storm.

But this would be different.

We owned the storm.

"Let's blow a hole in those bastards," I growled, eyes

fixed on the sickly green hull, thinking of the swarms inside.

They waited for the go ahead to surge through over the squadrons like locusts.

Nothing had been able to penetrate a Xathi hiveship before. They just plowed through and destroyed whatever they wanted, the swarms mopping up whatever the hiveship missed.

The Valorni, as annoying as they were, were inducted into the alliance for one reason. The Sugavians had worked with K'ver scientists using codialite, a mineral from the Valorni homeworld, to make one last attempt.

Just enough had been mined for this last-ditch effort —an experimental weapon that had a shot at penetrating that hull. It was rare, and we were on the losing end of this fight. We only had one shot.

We'd better make it count.

Every Skotan, K'ver, and Valorni warrior on the *Vengeance* had volunteered in the knowledge that it was a one-way trip. If this worked, the three strike teams below would board the Xathi and battle until there was nothing left.

If it didn't, we'd all die—just sooner.

Either way, the recorder satellites would beam the results of the experiment back to the scientists and engineers. We'd succeed, or they'd build a better weapon next time. That was the most important part of the mission, and we all understood how expendable we were.

The three of us locked focus on our stations as we crept closer.

"We are now in firing range, Captain," Sk'lar reported.

"Fire at will," was the only response.

Karzin sent the signal to the Valorni ships, and I started a slow count.

One.

His comrades had fought stupidly but bravely. There was no discernable pattern to the attack.

I was worried more would take friendly fire than would hit the Xathi, but they somehow made sense of the chaos, dodging fire from their comrades. If any survived the battle, they deserved to escape.

Two.

More likely the crazy bastards would follow us into the breach, but they'd earned the choice.

Three.

I activated the launch panel and braced, eyes fixed on the monitors. The adrenaline rushed through me in anticipation of the blow.

Nothing.

Not a bang or a pop or a whine. Just the hum of the

engines, and the wall of the Xathi ship growing larger on the screens.

The anticipation deflated as I looked at the panel in confusion. The damn thing was experimental, but it should at least fire. The engineers weren't brain-dead.

With a snarl, I slapped it again.

And then the universe turned inside out.

JENEVA

I was in my element.

I was where I belonged.

Completely alone in the silence, except for the gigantic bipedal tree creature with an affinity for spewing poison.

Home sweet home.

A glob of the foul stuff hissed as it ate away the earth beneath me. It was only inches from my boot, but I didn't flinch or try to move out of the way.

A rapid movement around a sorvuc was far more dangerous than its projectile poison. Its damn branches were covered in tiny neural fibers, capable of detecting incredibly small movements. The fibers were illuminated purple.

The sorvuc searched for me.

Under different circumstances, I would have found

it beautiful, but at that moment, it was just a pain in my ass.

The humidity made my short hair damp and scratchy. It clung to the curve of my neck. I longed to brush it away, but a movement like that would be a death sentence.

The luminescent purple faded away to a tranquil pink. I realized I was holding my breath.

Slowly, so slowly, I crept closer to the wide trunk of the sorvuc. I had already made an incision in its trunk. That's what pissed it off in the first place.

A necessary risk, but I only needed a few more drops of the thick scarlet fluid that seeped from the incision. The right person would pay a small fortune for its sap—or is it blood? Hell if I know.

As I slid my vial into place, ready to collect the liquid the sale of which would keep me comfortable for months, shouts erupted from somewhere nearby.

Damn it.

The sorvuc shrieked, its neural fibers flaring purple once again. It pivoted, razor-sharp leaves dangerously close to me. I rolled away, camouflaging my own movements in its rustling.

The hulking creature lumbered off in the direction the shouts came from—sort of. Its neural fibers must have picked up the sound vibrations, but with so many trees, it would have been difficult for the creature to determine the exact direction.

It's a good thing sorvuc had those fibers. They were as deaf as, well, a tree—at least, the sort of trees our ancestors brought over on their generation ship. But those trees sure as hell didn't fling poison or walk.

Walking plants were something the dense forest of Ankau had in excess. Even so, I'd take a hostile tree giant over people any day. At least they left me in peace.

Another round of shouts echoed through the trees. I clenched my teeth.

Speaking of peace.

I moved quickly and quietly through the dense forest, mindful not to disturb any of the thick vines that crisscrossed the forest floor. It was difficult to tell which ones were looking for a snack.

I spied a small herd of luurizi grazing between the roots of the docile Lenaus trees.

Their coats of lilac, sage, and pearl shimmered when they caught the mottled light bleeding through the canopy. Their silvery horns shone like jewels. It was easy to forget how deadly they were.

I was sure they could smell me.

Ordinarily, they would attack the moment they sensed an intruder. But this particular herd had become accustomed to my scent after so many years. It was an uneasy truce, but I still knew better than to take my eye off them.

Another bout of shouting brought me back to the present. It was louder this time. And stupider.

Clearly, whoever it was had a death wish, which was fine. I'd just prefer to be farther away when it happened.

The trees gave way to a small clearing. Two women, who I can only assume are the shouting morons, stood inches away from each other, their faces red with anger. They didn't notice my intrusion.

"You're not even trying anymore!" One woman, blonde and petite, hissed at the other. Her voice was tight, like she was trying to stay in control.

Sharp would have been the only way to describe her —sharp cheekbones, sharp chin, and sharp shoulders. Even her mouth was a sharp slash across her face.

I winced at her words, a headache throbbing at my temples. I almost wished something *would* come along and kill them.

"What more do you want me to do?" The other woman, dark-haired and softer than the other, answered wearily. "If I had known you were going to bring this up, I never would have agreed to meet you!"

Though they were different in coloring, they had the same nose and face shape. I guessed they were sisters—not that I cared.

"What other reason would there be to meet up?" the blonde snapped, her gray-green eyes narrowing. "What else do we have anymore?"

There was more poison in those words than there was in a fully grown sorvuc.

"I hate to interrupt," I said, startling both women.

I wanted to sound as annoyed as I felt, but my voice was brittle and raspy with disuse. I couldn't even remember the last time I had spoken aloud.

"But you really should shut up," I continued.

The blonde pivoted to face me. I was at least a head taller than her, but she somehow seemed bigger than she actually was. And the glare on her face would have made a narrisiri hesitate.

"This is none of your business," she said through clenched teeth.

"Nope, it isn't. I don't want to know about it. I don't care about it. But you really should find somewhere else to finish your screaming match," I replied.

"Do you think we're idiots? We have a howler with us," the blonde smugly fished a small black device from her pocket.

I hated those damn things. They emitted a high-pitched sound above the threshold of human hearing. It was meant to repel the creatures that stalked the forest, but I always thought it was a scam.

First of all, the people living in the cities and towns

hardly knew anything about the creatures that lived out here in the forest. Second, how would anyone know for a fact that a howler was working? No one could hear it.

"Yes, I do think you're idiots if you think that carrying a howler into the middle of aramirion territory during nesting season is a good idea," I snapped, fighting the urge to give the blonde a smug smile. "If they can hear that thing, you're screwed."

The dark-haired woman paled as she put her hand on the blonde's shoulder. The blonde stiffened at her touch.

"Leena, is that true?" the dark-haired woman whispered. Her eyes, the same color as the blonde's, nervously scanned the surrounding forest.

"How the hell would I know, Mariella? You're the one who moved all the way out to the middle of freaking nowhere!" the blonde, Leena, grumbled.

I turned to leave. Obviously, they had no intention of listening to me. Perhaps the dark-haired one, Mariella, might have seen reason, but Leena had some sort of chip on her shoulder—a chip the size of a damn ravine.

Fine. Whatever. They were adults.

I'd tried my best to warn them. It's not my fault if they chose not to listen to me.

What would I know, right? I've only been living out here for fifteen years. They would come to their senses and leave, or they would keep at it until one beast or another silenced them.

Either way, I got my forest and my silence back.

I could still feel their flurries of emotion as I marched through the undergrowth. If I was going to find another sorvuc to fill my vial, I needed to concentrate, but I couldn't do that with the feelings of two idiots in my head. I should turn back, try even harder to get them to leave.

A horrible screech unlike anything I had ever heard tore through the air. The sheer force of it drove me to my knees.

I tried to protect my ears with my hands, but it was useless. My vision blurred, stars danced behind my eyelids. I could practically feel my brain thrashing, desperate to escape that terrible sound.

Those idiots either did something to their howler, or the damn thing was malfunctioning. That had to be it.

As soon as I could get back on my feet, I staggered back to the clearing where I'd left the arguing pair. I would tear their stupid howler apart with my bare hands if I had to—anything to stop the noise.

"What the hell did you do?" I yelled.

Again, they didn't notice me when I entered the clearing, but, this time, they weren't distracted by an argument.

They stood side by side, looking up at the sky. Their faces were pale and their mouths were open in terror and confusion. I followed their gaze.

A jagged scar of pitch marred the once pristine stretch of endless blue.

The sky, *my* sky, had been torn open.

There was a beat of silence as if the whole planet had drawn in a collective breath of shock.

Then the forest erupted into chaos.

VREHX

Alarms blared around us. On the screen, all I could see were swirls of colors swallowing the Xathi.

The captain shouted orders to the rest of the crew, but his voice was distorted. It was changing—high-pitched then low and deep, fast then robotic, child-like then old, clear and loud, then soft and unintelligible.

Looking around the bridge, some of the colors were vibrant, glowing, and bright. Others were non-existent, as if all color had been drained, leaving behind various shades of gray.

Karzin's face twisted, melting down toward his midsection. I wanted to vomit, but Karzin's bird-like voice was chirping at me.

"TURN! IT! OFF!"

I turned my attention back to my control panel, just

to see it swirl around and fade. The screen was so bright, my eyes burned. The letters seemed to be dancing an old Skotan wedding march.

Looking up at the screen, the Xathi ship was ripped apart by the swirling vortex—no, it wasn't a vortex.

It was just a hole. Then it was a rip.

The only thing that stayed the same were the colors. Purple, white, and red streaks of color were covering the Xathi ship and reaching out for us.

The part of the Xathi ship already inside the rip was separating, coming apart at the seams. I could see part of the Xathi crew floating in space, then shredded by the force of the rip.

And we were getting closer to it.

I heard Rouhr's voice yelling out commands, for the engine room to go full speed ahead and drive the Xathi ship further into the rip.

It made sense. If the rip was doing this kind of damage to the "top" half, then it should destroy the rest of it as well. If we went with it, so be it.

The engines kicked in, and we were rocked forward as we crashed the *Vengeance* into the Xathi ziggurat. Our momentum pushed the Xathi ship further into the rip, and I watched as more and more of their vessels were ripped and disintegrated. It was only a few short breaths before the *Vengeance* herself began to fall through.

The energy inside her was incredible. The air carried a charge that made my scales tighten and my hair stand on end. Every color I had ever seen exploded in my eyes, bringing me a level of pain I had never felt before.

My mouth opened to scream, but no sound came out. It was as if my throat was burning and ripping in half vertically. I felt my skin and scales peel away from my body, exposing my muscles and bones to the emptiness of the void.

My eyelids, clamped as tight as I could hold them, broke apart and fell away, slowly exposing my eyes to the grayness of the void we had entered.

The bridge of the *Vengeance* was a bright gray, and everything else was varying shades of gray, getting darker and darker.

I looked at Rouhr to see his body falling apart like sand. He was yelling at us, but there was no sound.

That's when I realized that there was no sound at all. There wasn't a single solitary noise. Was the rip in space this quiet or had my ears been destroyed?

I moved my hand to touch my ear and stared in wonder at the stump at the end of my arm. I looked down, and my fingers were on my lap.

I wanted to retch. I wanted to die. I wanted to close my damn eyes.

I looked up at the screen to see the ziggurat, at least

the second half that we were attached to, reconstitute itself. It was rebuilding!

Then we were rebuilding, and the first of my senses to return was feeling. The pain was so much that I should have blacked out, except my eyelids weren't there.

When they finally returned, and I blinked for the first time, tears fell down my face. Finally, sound came back with an explosion of noise.

"...the hell is happening?"

"...are we?"

"Damage reports!"

"...off the damn switch."

"...switch, Vrehx!"

It felt as though forever was passing before my mind caught on to what they were wanting. I looked at my control panel and flipped the switch to the weapon. The void ended, and the alarms were back.

"Where the hell are we?" Rouhr asked.

"I'm not sure, Captain!" Sk'lar answered.

"Scan the—" Rouhr was interrupted as the ship shook violently, knocking most of us from our seats. "By all that is holy, what was that?"

Engineer Thribb's voice came on over the intercom. "We're losing engines, Captain. Partial power only. We've been caught by a gravitational field of some sort."

"What is generating the field?"

"I'm not sure, sir. My systems are inoperative."

"Sk'lar!"

"On it!" Sk'lar checked his system, letting out a curse that the translator didn't bother to translate. There was no need. "We're above a planet. Unfortunately, we are falling toward it."

He tried to keep his voice calm, but the slight vibrato betrayed his emotions.

The *Vengeance* wasn't built for the atmosphere of a planet. Our thrusters wouldn't work. If we fell into the atmosphere of a planet, we'd fall until we impacted with the ground, and it would be a very hard landing.

"Sir! The Xathi!" I called out, pointing at the screen.

The Xathi ziggurat was tilting, as if it were falling as well. Outside scanners adjusted and brought the full picture into view.

The planet was covered in green and blue, and above it, the Xathi ship tilted ever more as it fell.

"What planet is this, and where are the Xathi going to land?" Rouhr asked.

I brought up our positioning and the star maps in our database. "Sir, this is uncharted space for us. We don't have this planet or this system in our database."

Rouhr nodded, absorbing the information. "Crash site?"

Sk'lar turned to look at me, then at Rouhr. The look

on his face was silent resignation that something bad was going to happen.

"There appear to be seven main points of population on the planet. The Xathi are going to crash into the biggest concentration," Sk'lar said.

"Estimated survival?"

"Not good. Easily half of their city will be destroyed, killing thousands."

"And what of the Xathi? Will they survive the crash?"

"I'm not sure, sir. I'm not sure what the interior makeup of their vessel is, so I couldn't give you an accurate guess," Sk'lar replied, refusing to look at Rouhr as he stared at the computer.

"Engineer Thribb?"

"Captain?"

"Any chance of us breaking free and *not* crashing on the planet below?"

"Less than three percent, sir."

"Well, *groop*." We all looked at Rouhr in shock. "Any way to get us away from civilization?"

"Easily, as long as our engines don't finish cutting out on the way down."

"Then keep us away from any population centers. The rest of you, brace for impact!"

We watched the Xathi ziggurat crash into the center

city, the largest city, as we strapped ourselves into our seats.

The cloud of dust and flame took out half of our sensors as we entered the atmosphere. We gained speed and tilted forward, and I could feel the pressure of the straps trying to hold me up as gravity pulled me downward.

It was a struggle to breathe. The pull of gravity was forcing us downward, while the atmosphere tried to resist our penetration. I tried to lift my arm to my console to push the button for the retro rockets in order to level us out and slow us down, but I couldn't lift my arm high enough.

The ground rushed at us, and I closed my eyes.

I'll be back with you soon, my family, I thought. My only hope was that we took those bastards with us.

My head snapped forward as the *Vengeance* crashed into the ground.

There was no way that death could possibly hurt this much.

I looked to my left to see Karzin slowly and gingerly lifting his head. Just past him, S'toz's head hung forward, his chin on his chest. To my right, Sk'lar was moaning in pain, trying to reach his arm up to his head.

I slowly—oh, so, so slowly reached up to unbuckle my straps. Now free from my restraints—and oh so grateful for them, as well—I gingerly got to my feet, waiting for the blast of pain to overwhelm my senses.

"Location?" I asked.

Sk'lar answered after a short coughing fit. "We're planet-side. That's all I know. Last thing I remember seeing was that we were heading for a large forest."

That's when it finally hit me. The computers were down.

"Captain?"

A groan from behind Sk'lar answered us. Rouhr's straps had snapped, and he ended up being flung around.

"I'm still alive. Vrehx?" He pulled himself to a sitting position on the floor, his right arm dangling, blood flowing from his cheek, and his left arm clutching his ribs.

"Sir?" My left arm hurt, and it was hard to breathe, I might have cracked a rib or six. I had a headache from the depths of destruction, and I was struggling to maintain weight on my right ankle.

"Get the commanders and your teams together. Find out where we are and if we're in danger. Thribb and I will handle the ship."

I knew better than to argue with him.

I made my way to the lift, but the doors wouldn't open.

I moved three steps to my left and opened the maintenance hatch. Looking down, it was surprisingly clear.

Time to climb, I thought.

At least it was downward.

Click to get Vrehx now!

https://elinwynbooks.com/conquered-world-alien-romance/

NEED TO CATCH UP WITH THE STAR BREED?

Given: Star Breed Book One

When a renegade thief and a genetically enhanced mercenary collide, space gets a whole lot hotter!

Thief Kara Shimsi has learned three lessons well - keep her head down, her fingers light, and her tithes to the syndicate paid on time.

But now a failed heist has earned her a death sentence - a one-way ticket to the toxic Waste outside the dome. Her only chance is a deal with the syndicate's most ruthless enforcer, a wolfish mountain of genetically-modified muscle named Davien.

The thought makes her body tingle with dread-or is it heat?

Mercenary Davien has one focus: do whatever is necessary to get the credits to get off this backwater mining colony and back into space. The last thing he wants is a smart-mouthed thief - even if she does have the clue he needs to hunt down whoever attacked the floating lab he and his created brothers called home.

Caring is a liability. Desire is a commodity. And love could get you killed.

https://elinwynbooks.com/star-breed/

ABOUT THE AUTHOR

I love old movies – *To Catch a Thief, Notorious, All About Eve* — and anything with Katherine Hepburn in it. Clever, elegant people doing clever, elegant things.

I'm a hopeless romantic.

And I love science fiction and the promise of space.

So it makes perfect sense to me to try to merge all of those loves into a new science fiction world, where dashing heroes and lovely ladies have adventures, get into trouble, and find their true love in the stars!

www.ingramcontent.com/pod-product-compliance
Lightning Source LLC
LaVergne TN
LVHW020041110826
845155LV00029B/589

* 9 7 8 1 9 4 0 9 2 4 6 9 4 *